The Demon Inside Me

This is a work of fiction. All of the characters, organizations, and events portrayed in this novel are either works of fiction or are used fictitiously.

ISBN - 9798872521761

Copyright © 2024

by Stephen W. Scott

Book cover design by Derek Stewart

"The Demon Inside Me"

by

Stephen W. Scott

A huge thanks to the following for their help: Derek Stewart for his wonderful cover design and his creativity in my promotional videos. Also, a big thanks to podcasters Alex Edwards for helping promote the book, and Brian Sammons for his advice and help along this journey. Finally, my greatest appreciation for my Writing Coach and Editor, Heather Nuttall-Westover.

TABLE OF CONTENTS

Paranoic Personality

Nauseated, I gagged. Painful coughs erupted and my blurry vision became worse when sweat dripped from my forehead. The ringing in my ears was jarring, and it echoed endlessly. Something punched my gut from the inside. Pain fired through my joints – mostly my knees, elbows, and shoulders, making me grunt. My neck hurt just to move it. "Help me." My voice, scratchy and rough, hurt so much there was barely any volume left. It felt like I had been yelling for hours.

Images of terrifying pale hands with fleshy, rough skin tried to grab me. The long fingers, black, twisted, and scaly, disgusted me. Behind them, hideous blackened eyes set back underneath massive foreheads. Their jagged, rotting teeth, had black slime over the discolored gum lines. I shut my eyes, only to see them longer. I covered my ears to stop the annoying vibrations. That did not help, either.

Voices called my name. Not the subtle, angry ones. These sounded human.

"I think it's gone," said a feminine voice.

"Is it the boy?" The unfamiliar voice confused me.

"Jeffrey – can you hear me?"

Happy to hear that voice, I whispered, "Father Matthew?"

"Yes, Jeffrey." He smiled – but it seemed forced and insincere. He was always nice but seemed a bit off. His hands ran through his short, red hair. The tough, lean face, spotted with bruises, looked worried. Dark sunglasses shielded his eyes – but it was because Father Matthew was blind. Strangely, he could see so much better than most people. He was the most amazing priest I'd ever known.

"Jefferey," he said, hugging me, "it's gone, but he could come back at any second."

"What the fuck?" I knew I shouldn't cuss in front of a priest, but the dull pain hurt with every move. Only in boxers, I was freezing. Is that why I was shaking uncontrollably? Or was it out of terror?

"Jeffrey, I am Father Bradley. Tell me, do you remember anything?" The older priest had a rounder face that also had a few bruises and cuts. Sweat rolled down his forehead. How was he so hot when I felt so cold? He said something in Latin and crossed my forehead, sprinkling holy oil and water.

Something lurched in me. A loud guttural scream burst forth. Wow! My own breath made me gag. Jumping to my feet, a second scream exploded. A chill seized my skin and dug in deep to my tendons, muscles, and bones.

"Jeffrey," said Sister Regina, "try to pray with me." Cuts and dry blood marred her pretty face. Her wrists had bruises as if someone grabbed her violently. "Our Father, who art in heaven …" Sister Regina's voice lost her calmness. She seemed to be holding back tears.

The dark, cold thing in my chest exploded, spreading to my heart, mind, and limbs. It fused with my muscles, my bones, and my soul. Loud, afraid, and angry, it bellowed inside me. Another explosion of the thing sent me to my feet. A rage swirled in my mind. Everything suddenly had a red tint to it. I had no control! Unable to stop, I pushed Father Matthew into the wall. Next, I kicked Sister Regina so hard; she bled heavily out of her mouth and nose. How could I do that? I loved them. Father Matthew and Sister Regina were almost like family. They were always there for me. Why couldn't I stop attacking them?

An invisible force squeezed my lungs. Cold, it spread into my spine and ribs – stretching them. I struggled for breath. My spine stretched. How could I be … floating? I was in midair!

I grabbed Father Matthew and lifted him by his neck. How could I do that? What held me up? My other hand ripped pages out of his Bible. My vision faded as this new personality emerged again. It spit on Father Bradley and then threw him back into the wall. It celebrated within me while casting contempt at the priests.

Caught in a Dream

Its face glared at me. Although it had various forms, the … thing had three favorites. This one was the worst. Did it know of the jolting terror it triggered? The reddish, burnt, and bubbling skin pulsed. Puss leaked from some of the blisters and reeked of something like the chlorine I had to put in the pool at the motel Mom managed. The eyes did not exist. Two black, large, sunken orbs faded into nothing. The lips had sinewy strips of flesh that stretched as it opened its mouth, releasing swarms of gnats, flies, and misshapen, mutant hornets.

The disgusting insects surrounded my head – some leaving stings, while others tried to irritate my ears, eyes, and nostrils. Afraid, I kept my mouth shut tight, and flailed my hands to swat and push away the creepy things that buzzed their wings near my head.

Everything disappeared. Sighing, I felt a comforting peace. Although it was small, gratefulness inspired me to cross myself. A small amount of light penetrated the window, the blinds, and the curtains. It felt warm and soothing.

Glancing around, I realized it was my room. The trophies from minibike competitions, and action figures from all my favorite horror movies decorated my shelves: Jason Voorhees, Michael Myers, Pinhead, Pennywise, and Chucky. My autographed pictures with Kane Hodder, Nick Castle, and Robert Englund all hung on my wall, along with my fan art from old and popular movies like "Halloween," "Dawn of the Dead," "Friday the 13th", to modern movies like "The Conjuring" and "It."

On my shelves were the books that embedded themselves within me. I perfectly arranged my books by HP Lovecraft, Dan Simmons, Richard Matheson, and Stephen King along with classics like "Frankenstein," "Dr. Jekyll and Mr. Hyde," and "Dracula."

What appealed to me most, however, were the pictures on my desk. My cousin, Gunner, posed with me on my minibike in the picture to the left. The picture to the right was Elise with her arm around me. She had simple dark hair that moved to the right, and she wore glasses that made her look smart. Of course, she didn't smile. She could be annoying as hell – especially with her sick, twisted sense of humor. However, we loved each other. Twins usually do – although we were fraternal.

Mom and Dad were in the other picture. Dad wore jeans stained with oil and grease, and an oversized

Motley Crue T-Shirt. His eyes bulged as if afraid, and his mouth had formed a circle surrounded by his long brown-grayish beard. Mom's eyes, exaggerated, displayed a crazed look, and she had a dirty wrench reared back. The smile on her face countered the pretend anger. I wanted to smile at every image, but I could not find any joy connected to those old memories. All my hope had contracted so tight and become so cold, it could not escape.

Light faded fast as an ominous, low growl made me shudder. The hot breath poured on the back of my neck. It howled. I turned around to see it, but it disappeared. Just barely out of my sight, I kept turning on myself. Spinning, I kept going in and out of the light. In and out. Light and dark. In and out. Light and dark. Confused, dizzy, I stopped to take a deep breath.

"Jeffrey. Jeffrey. Can you hear us?"

Their words twisted, changed, echoed, and slowed. Somehow, I understood what they said. "Yes. I hear you. Please, help me. Help me get out of here."

"Where are you? What do you see?"

"I'm in my room." Something shot behind my back. It jumped to the left. Again, I kept trying to see it. "There's something in here. It's circling me. But I can't see it. Please help me. Make it go away. Please!" My voice bounced, hollowing out with every reverberation. It sounded as if I was in a canyon, or perhaps a cave.

I saw it in my closet-door mirror! The … thing stood behind me. Father Matthew and Bradley stood in front of me. How could I not see them in front of me as opposed to the mirror? How could I not see the creature behind me?

I turned around again, and the room spun in the opposite direction,

Father Matthew and … I forgot his name … tried to talk but their voices distorted, slowed, and stretched. Their faces looked dead – like zombies. Their eyes never blinked. The motions of their arms slowed and froze like a statue.

My ears cringed at the foreign language that echoed loudly, even vibrating through my ribs. My eyes shut as tight as I could while my hands covered my ears.

Something took over again, pushing my will aside. I growled. Slobber sprayed on the priests and nun. Why couldn't I move? I felt locked in place. Sweat pushed through my pores continuously, although my room felt like a refrigerator. Their breaths formed a misty cloud that faded as it fell on me. Sister Regina put some blankets over me.

My whole body writhed, and my skin felt like fire once again as the other priest sprinkled something on me. The voice in my head screamed so loud it felt like my eardrum would rupture. The room suddenly twisted in another direction, as if it was trying to keep me in the shadows.

The voice exploded once again within. Why won't it leave? My whole body stretched and heaved as if I was throwing up. My elbows, shoulders, hips, knees, and ankles felt so much stress. What's happening to me? The ugly presence vanished, taking all my strength. My knees dropped to the floor, and I fell to the side.

"Father Matthew," I sounded normal. My heart raced. I quivered. I managed to mutter in between my heavy breaths, "…how long … how long has this …" I grunted, "been … going on?" My voice sounded demonic – stretched, low, and spread out.

"Three months."

Shit! Never in my life was I so confused. It reminded me of the time I had that Covid crap during the Pandemic. That was just for three or four days. But three months? I wanted out of this place. There was no track of time. Elements of my physical world like my room and house mixed with horrid images, shadows, smells, and sounds of nightmares.

Corners of the room slipped, locked, and reformed. It twisted, causing a huge cold gust of wind. Images, memories of Elise, Mom, Dad, Gunner all flashed through my mind. Something smelled like spoiled, rotting meat. I pulled a blanket tight for warmth and lifted the corner to cover my nose.

Hunger pains punched my stomach from inside. I wanted to venture downstairs to the kitchen. I wanted my favorite breakfast: waffles, scrambled eggs, and bacon. I thought of going to Mom or Elise's room. However, I remembered those rooms had disappeared into a dark, blank void a while ago. Keeping the blanket over me, I opened my bedroom door.

The rush of heat – lifting from a gaping hole, mixed with a harsh wind. A subtle red glow lifted, carrying random sparks. Almost too hot to breathe, it reminded me of that summer Dad and Mom took me and Elise to Arizona to see the Grand Canyon. From the pit, some stifled moans, screams, and wails tried to escape. A few sparks provided a faint, yet distinct outline of the thing. It perched on the railing. Immense, it appeared larger than the last time. Or was I smaller? I examined the head, the elongated ears, folded wings, and large shoulders. The arms extended and pointed at me. It then pointed to the pit below. An emptiness fell through me. Hollowed out, I knew I was destined for the pit.

"Please let me go. Please." The heat evaporated my tears. "I just wanna be with my mom and my sister."

It did not growl or snort at me. Silent, its head shook.

"Who are you?" I screamed, "and what do you want from me?" My words devolved into sobbing.

Again, I looked for a way to escape. The darkness fell like a heavy drape, blocking out all light. It dropped closer. The downstairs was gone. I could only walk on the upper landing but not far. The house contracted, shrinking bit by bit. How much longer until it swallowed me? When would I cease to exist? When would that thing take over?

There was no way out. Is this place real? Was this in my mind? Is it a dream? If so – why couldn't I wake up? Where was Mom, Elise, Father Matthew, and Sister Regina? How'd I get here? My mind drifted back as far as it could. Slowly, the memories returned, forming pictures, conversations, and revelations. I needed to re-ground myself with the physical world and figure out what happened. I found the one prominent memory that stood out and let my mind focus on it.

Pain (four months ago)

Depressing rain filled my insides, drowning my stomach in sadness. The floodwaters lifted to my heart, neck, then my eyes acted like spillways, allowing tears to escape. Mom hugged me. So did Elise. They cried, too, as Dad's coffin dropped into the cold, dry ground.

For the last few days – it seemed so unreal. It felt distant, as if his death had not really happened. I kept thinking of texting him on the phone, or rather calling him to talk to him. However, reality dropped just like the casket – except it fell harder and heavier. The truth had a cold, blunt presence, like the north November wind. It almost toppled me to the ground.

Taking a huge breath, I managed to push the depression away – but only for a split second. The truth returned, punching my stomach, causing more tears to escape. For the last few days, I felt numb, as if it wasn't real. Today, I realized Dad was gone for good.

Father Matthew said a prayer. I heard it – but didn't hear it. The ugly turmoil within my chest distracted me from the words. Disconnected, I had no understanding of what he said. All I could think of was the grave taking Dad from me.

People started lining up and passing in front. I was the first person the other mourners met. All of them had somber faces, saddened eyes, and a faded light that came from used, weak batteries. Uncle Walt, Aunt Beth, then Gunner passed by, each one offering me a hug. Gunner's tight grip pulled me so close. He was my first and best friend. Only a year younger, he was like a brother instead of a cousin.

Next, Mom's sister, Aunt Janet, passed by with Uncle Dan. I didn't know them well. They were from Albany. Justin was their son, and Jason was the nephew they adopted after his parents and brother died somewhere in Brazil. I think it was a car wreck that also rendered Jason blind.

More people came to shake my hand and tell me how sorry they were – or how much they loved Dad. I was not too sure if I heard them – much like the prayer Father Matthew said a little while ago.

I glanced at the grave briefly. My eyes caught a glimpse of the tombstone: Jason Michael McPherson. Husband, Father, and Son. Born October 31, 1974, Died November 10, 2023. I averted the sight, hoping it might change reality.

The slapping noise erupted through the house. "I wish you'd show some goddamned emotions and have a little respect for your father and me. He just died! When you say shit like that it hurts!" Mom's tirade disintegrated into sobs.

"Jesus, Elise," I mumbled to myself. "What the hell did you just say to Mom now?" I rolled my eyes – even though Sis was not here. I wanted to slap her, myself.

Gunner sighed. "Your sister's a bitch."

I nodded, then reclined, and stared at the ceiling. "You've told me that a thousand times." Neither of us wanted to play any video games or wrestle. We just stared at the ceiling.

"I'm really gonna miss your dad, too," said Gunner. "Mostly because he liked the things I liked: horror movies, comic books, and scary books." Gunner cried. "I loved him more than my own dad. And I love the way your dad told those scary stories." He chuckled amidst his crying. "And I'll never forget the time he snuck upon us with the pantyhose on his head. Scared the living shit out of me."

A sad smile broke across my face. "I'm really gonna miss working on engines with him." The smile vanished. "I can't go hunting with him again. Or play catch with

Dad or go to the movies. Gunner – I'm worried. Will we have enough money to live on? And then, will I need to get a job to help Mom and take care of her and Elise?"

"Elise doesn't need to be helped. She needs to be committed to a mental hospital – and be put in the strongest ward. She scares me."

I grinned. "Dude, it was a joke." You'd think he'd get it by now that she does that to prank people: the stoic look, the dark clothing, and the way she said things. Elise reminded the whole family of Wednesday Addams. She relished the comparison, embraced the role, and rarely ever broke character. She had a hobby of researching serial killers and would give speeches on how she would rank them as a skilled psychotic murderer.

I grinned, thinking about the awesome Halloween prank Elise and I played on Gunner. He was still spooked about it . . .

I hid behind the table. Gunner and Elise entered the cold shed. Gunner wore his golden Pittsburgh Steelers hoodie. Pulling down the hood, you could see his lean face framed with that sandy-brown hair that parted on the left. His face and colors lit up the shed. His nose was straight and lean, and his blue eyes were less round – making him look confident and strong. A lot of girls at school thought he was "hot." If they only knew how awkward he felt when having to wear those skimpy competition swimsuits at swim meets.

Elise, on the other hand, robbed light. It was because of her black Slipknot Sweatshirt, and her black hair and dark eyes. She also painted her fingernails black.

Irritated, Gunner sighed. "Now what is it, Elise? What is it you're so desperate to talk about?"

She pointed up to the rafters at the owl's nest. "See that nest."

Gunner pointed too. "That one or the one on the far rafter?"

Before he knew it, Elise slapped the handcuffs on his wrist and snapped the other cuff to the metal support beam. He cussed, turned towards that hand, then she used the other cuffs to snatch the free wrist and secure it to the wooden support beam of the tool board.

I was about to burst into laughter, but I somehow held it in. I aimed my phone at him and Elise from an angle so you could see both their faces. "Damnit, Elise!" he yelled, "What the fuck are you doing?"

She stood a few feet away from him. Her face showed no emotion.

"Unlock these things now!" His voice tried to sound tough, but it had not begun to change. "Do you hear me?"

Elise quietly sat on a hay bale at a make-shift table where we often played cards, dice, and even messed with a Ouija Board. She set a little black box on the table. "Gunner, we must talk."

"About what? How you're a weird, crazy psycho? Let me out of these things, now!"

"Gunner," again she spoke with a straight face. "I heard your parents talking. They think you masturbate too much."

He turned red. I giggled silently, remembering when Elise walked in on him in the bathroom a few weeks ago. The idiot didn't think to lock the door.

"I, myself, was appalled at your lack of self-control," she said while opening the black box, revealing the sharp, metal objects. She held the scalpel. "So, I have decided to surgically remove your penis and testicles."

I swallowed to contain my laughter as his face turned totally white and his eyes bulged wide. He gulped hard, gasped, then tugged the handcuffs while his breath shortened into grunts.

Elise showed him the hypodermic needle. How can she not burst out laughing? She didn't even smile! How could she do that?

"Now this is your local anesthetic," she said. "It should work."

She approached Gunner as he tried to kick her away. "Stay away from me you psycho crazed bitch! Help! Jeffrey, help!"

I wheezed trying to bottle my laughter that turned into tears. I had to focus to keep the iPhone camera on him.

"Help! Uncle Jason! Aunt Jenny! Help! Someone!"

Elise finally got him to stop yelling. "Gunner. If you don't be quiet, I won't give you the anesthetic."

Gunner, crying, shook his head. "Please don't. Elise – please!"

"Gunner, you'll swim faster without a bulge down there."

Panicked, he yanked harder and yelled louder. "Help! Uncle Jason! Jeffrey!" He kicked at her but missed, falling backwards. He grunted hard as the cuffs jerked him to a stop. Vulnerable, Elise unbuttoned his pants and yanked them down. Only in his boxers and hoodie, he sobbed. "Elise, please don't. Please."

My chest almost burst from laughter when I saw him pee himself.

"Yuck," said Elise. "Gross. I guess we better clean you up." She plunged the syringe as it sprayed the water on his groin. "Happy Halloween, Gunner."

My laughter exploded all through my stomach, my chest, and my shoulders. Stumbling close with the camera, I found some control of my laughter that erupted. "Happy Halloween."

Gunner, petrified, shook his head violently. "That's not funny! That's not funny. It's not funny!"

Unfazed, serious, Sis unlocked his cuffs. Gunner fell, yanked up his pants and darted for the house. "Mom! Aunt Jenny! Uncle Jason!"

Mom was mega pissed. You could always tell because her head leaned to the left, a vein in her forehead was more prominent, and she pressed her lips together. Her voice was taut, short, and sharp. Dad nodded, while holding his mouth and beard as Gunner told the story of what happened. Dad burst out laughing from his belly and chest. Mom first poked him, then glared furiously. Dad washed his smile away, hiding it under his beard. "I'm sorry. That's …" he started laughing again, "funny. I'm sorry," he said holding up his hands. "It's sadistic and twisted – but it IS funny." He had a raspy voice, but it was somehow friendly and inviting. It made anyone want to listen – and it was perfect for telling stories.

"Jason!" Mom glared at Dad.

Dad, scared of Mom, straightened up, and washed his smile away. "You're mother's right. That joke – while funny – was inappropriate to play on your cousin." I did my best not to smile when Dad shielded his lips from Mom and mouthed the word, "HILARIOUS."

Mom held out her hand. "Your phones. Give them to me."

"Ah, Mom," I said. "It's just a Halloween prank."

"Traumatizing your cousin is NOT a prank!"

I flinched at Mom's angry voice. Her cold, short words felt like sharp teeth biting me. I quickly surrendered my phone.

"And no minibike for two weeks."

I winced as that punishment hurt far worse than losing my phone. "It was all Lizzy Borden's idea," I said while pointing at Elise.

Mom glared now at Elise. "Your phone, NOW!"

Elise let out a frustrated sigh and gave Mom her phone. "Thanks a lot, Mother," she said in her usual emotionless voice. "I wasted all last week reading on how to perform this surgery. I was so looking forward to castrating him and putting the parts in an alcohol filled jar in my room as a trophy."

"Do either of you have anything to say to your cousin?" Dad's voice, quiet and reserved, nudged me.

Aunt Beth hugged Gunner who shook uncontrollably. Terror washed through his eyes – making me feel kinda bad. Maybe we did go too far. Embarrassed, I could not face my cousin. "Gunner ... I ... I ..."

Dad touched my shoulder. "Look people in the eye when apologizing."

I nodded, then looked at Gunner's scared eyes. "I'm sorry, dude." We always called each other dude because Dad said that's how guys talked in the 1980s.

"Elise," said Mom, "what should you say to your cousin?"

Her head turned. "Gunner, I apologize for not being clear to you in the shed. I would've only removed one testicle and let you keep the other one."

Returning to the present, regret had me shaking my head, but I still managed to chuckle.

"Dude – that wasn't funny!" Gunner protested. "I've had nightmares about that. She was dead serious. I can't believe you helped her!"

"Gunner, all I did was shoot the video." I laughed. "And I would've stopped her if she really tried it."

As usual Uncle Walt and Aunt Beth were livid. My uncle threatened to sue Elise and me. He was a bunch of hot air. He was always threatening to sue people. And he could never take a joke at his expense. Dad said his brother had his sense of humor surgically removed when he came out of the womb. Quite often, you did have to explain a joke to Uncle Walt. As a college professor, he buried his head into books so much he had no connection with regular people. He ridiculed Dad for the horror movies and his vast collection of horror movie memorabilia. He also chided Aunt Beth for her collection of Movie Musical Posters. Gunner didn't like it when his dad made fun of him for loving superhero comics and Star Wars.

Freddy jumped on the bed between us. My beagle dog, named after Freddy Kruger, looked at me, barked, and dropped the tennis ball next to me. "Not today, boy." I pet him. Freddy licked my face, then Gunner's. His warm, wet tongue made me smile. Did he try to console us? Although he was the family dog, I did most of the feeding, played "fetch" with him, took him for walks, and he always slept in my bed. I think he was scared of Elise, though.

"Hey, kiddo."

Anger encouraged me to sit up in the bed and shoot a glare at her.

"You sick psycho." Gunner, still freaked by her prank, got up and moved away from her. His jaw quivered, and I saw tremors in his fingers. "Stay away from me." Boy, she really did traumatize him.

Elise stood in the doorframe. She wore dark jeans, and an AC/DC T-Shirt. That meant it was Thursday. The Slipknot T-Shirt was for Friday. Metallica was Monday, Radiohead was for Tuesday, and the Addams Family T-Shirt was for Wednesdays. Refusing to blink, my angry stare tried to push her back. She sat on the corner of my bed. Her arms and legs were so thin, they were like toothpicks. Some kids teased her about having an eating disorder, but I always told them to leave Elise alone. I could attest she ate a lot, but never gained one pound. Her dark eyes always had the glasses shield her from reality – or did they help her to see through the idiocy of others? She also had a very dark, yet intelligent sense of humor. She smiled for me – and Mom and Dad, but it was often on the left side of her face. She also had a smart look, which was accurate. She could plow through a book (sometimes two) in a week. Even some of her teachers thought she was weird. But weird is good, especially for my family.

"Hey kiddo, and future eunuch." referring to me and Gunner, respectively. "What are you thinking about? Life after death? What heaven is like? Or is dad just a stinking, rotting corpse that is food for a bunch of worms and other subterranean creatures?"

"Is that what you just said to Mom?" Her eyes dropped, showing a slight hint of regret. "You know, sis, you have a very twisted, and sick way of dealing with death. You better not say anything like that to Mom, again." My words shared the anger of my eyes. "And don't say anything like that to me, either. Dad's dead and you want to do your twisted act to amuse yourself, or make yourself feel oh-so-smart? Just for once, think about other peoples' feelings."

Embarrassed, she hesitated. "I'm sorry, kiddo. I just … don't know how to feel right now. I still can't believe it's real." For a change, some emotion crept into her voice, and in her dark eyes. I knew she had emotions and thoughts. I was one of the few people she expressed them to. Then, I saw it: a small, silvery tear streamed. "I just … don't know how to describe what I feel. I think Mom hates me for it."

Gunner relaxed. I do not think he had ever seen Elise show any emotion. He rubbed her shoulder. "I'm sorry, Elise. Really."

I gave her a hug. Elise pulled me so tight – like she never had before. My arms squeezed, too. For some reason, I felt better. "And quit calling me 'kiddo,'" I whispered. "We're the same age, and I was out of the womb first." My wit added, "I had to get away from you because you're so mega annoying."

"I miss him so much," she said. "I never thought I would – but I do. I keep thinking he's out in the shed either working on one of the cars or building something."

I already missed that because I was helping him with all the mechanical stuff. He'd say, "Get the three-sixteenth wrench. Or get the six-millimeter socket." I knew what they looked like. Our hands and fingers, covered in oil and dirt, dabbed unique shapes on each tool. We coded them to our hands and fingers that had small bruises, cuts, and calloused fingers. His hands would never touch mine again. We could never fix refrigerator motors, car engines, compressors for air conditioners, and pneumatic springs again. Dad could even repair my spirit when I had a sad day. "I'm gonna miss him so much. I'd do anything to get him back."

Talk Talk (With Mr. Owl)

The shed was quiet today. Gunner didn't come over to talk today because Uncle Walt didn't want him to come over as much. I got mad at my uncle for that. I was angrier at him for not crying about his brother's death. Dad admitted he and Uncle Walt were never close, and their personalities were diametrically opposed.

My thoughts went back to Dad. Usually in the shed, Dad and I laughed and talked. Now, the clinking of my tools with nuts and bolts didn't have conversation or laughter.

The intake manifold on my minibike needed adjustments. Also, my carburetor needed a new air filter. I wiped some sweat off my forehead, with my sleeve. Now, the sleeve wiped away a couple of tears. Dad often guided my hands in the mechanical tasks. The oils that stained our hands mixed along with our sweat. The dirtier our hands got, the more we felt connected. He wanted me to love riding the minibike just as much as he loved driving his truck.

I put a few more pieces of wood in the stove. The walls did not completely stop the north wind from carrying some harsh and cold air into the shed. It added to my sadness. "I miss you, Dad," I whispered. My voice was in the process of changing, but ever since Dad died, my voice sounded more like a boy. "I miss you so much." Could he hear me?

There it was again. My head turned. It seemed like something stayed just beyond my eyesight and ears. It had me spinning. I noticed the shadows, or rather the flickering of the flames in the stove dancing on the walls. No. Whatever moved now soared above me. A slight breeze hit me. I heard the fluttering of wings.

Looking high, I smiled for the first time in nearly two weeks. It was Mr. Owl, the Barn Owl who lived in our shed. His nest was at the peak of the roof on some rafters about 30 feet above me. He was like an old friend who watched us like a protector. Sometimes, we just talked, and the owl remained quiet like the friend who'd just listen to anyone rambling. Mr. Owl would nod his head as if agreeing with you. Sometimes Dad would ask, "Mr. Owl, how many licks does it take to get to the Tootsie Roll center roll of a Tootsie Pop?" That was the only time Mr. Owl would look at dad as if it was a stupid question.

I sprawled on my back on a bale of hay, smiled, and looked at him. I waved. He stared at me, tilted his head, and swiveled it a few times as if wondering about me. My smile faded. "Mr. Owl … I'm really sad. Dad died – you know. His truck broke down on the highway. He got out to put the reflectors on the road and when he was doing that – someone hit him. I really miss him." I didn't know what else to say – but then again, I was talking to an owl.

Mr. Owl had no words. His beady black eyes had a huge sense of curiosity. His head bowed, as if feeling sad. After he let out a few hoots and whimpers, I wished for a way to understand them. His head tilted left, then right, then back to the left as if listening to my story. Did he really know? Did Mr. Owl sense my sadness, and maybe express condolences? Did he miss Dad, too?

The empty, painful hunger in my stomach outmatched the pain in my chest. The carburetor will have to wait until tomorrow. I doused the fire in the stove with some ashes, causing the warmth and light to fade. It matched my whole being. I looked up. "Goodnight, Mister Owl." I turned out the light and watched the owl change from bright guardian to something sinister wrapped in shadow.

I stopped at the door to look back. I squinted at the darkness focusing on Mr. Owl's shiny, large eyes. Immediately I felt a nervous dread that punched my chest. For some reason, a tingling bubbled under my skin. It forced my lips to quiver, and my fingers to shake. Did something, other than Mr. Owl, watch me? The unseen eyes felt … sinister and hateful. I left urgently, hoping to leave the anxious fear behind.

Wake the Dead

My minibike was alive again! It sped across the terrain several hundred feet from the shed. The wind slapped through my helmet. Fortunately, the balaclava and my helmet offered some protection. As I contorted my body to keep balance with the machine, I worked up a sweat. Shit, now my facemask fogged a bit.

Pulling the clutch and kicking the gear, my minibike shifted up to third. The lurch to a higher speed excited me. I downshifted to avoid a dragging collision with a dirt mound, but I went back up to third gear then fourth – until the speed felt dangerous. I liked the danger. It made me feel alive. My heart sped, my mind raced, thinking of all the perils that could happen. I did not care about any of them.

Damnit – now my hair slipped out of the balaclava and partially blocked my vision. Mom would say, "Get it cut. You look like a sheep dog. How can you see anything with all that hair?"

Returning to the moment, I managed the bike on the uneven, natural, muddied terrain. It bumped up and down, side-to-side, but I knew how to keep myself even and stable. I downshifted while turning the handlebars sharp left. My back wheel slung about 90 degrees. I pivoted the handlebars a little and managed to turn around without stopping. I hope Gunner was getting a good shot of this on his phone.

Upshifting, I revved the engine and it burst forward with high speed. Everything around me was a blur. The cold, sporadic rain left a hard, cake-like residue. Fortunately, I never lost momentum.

Eying the mound, I gasped. My heart thumped faster. Dad and I built the mound – much to Mom's irritation. We used the earth and clay to make a four-foot ramp that supported me and the minibike. I loved flying for a split second. Hopefully this time, I will not crash.

I revved it as high as it could go as my front tire shot up the ramp. Before I could think "one," I sailed through the air for probably eight to ten feet, then fell back to the Earth. The jarring bounce was too hard. Although the shock absorbers flexed, my back and legs didn't, and I fell to the side into the slightly muddied ground. The impact sent my head onto a rock and jarred all the air out of my body. Several coughs tried to retrieve air back into my lungs, but all they did was trigger my head to pound – almost syncing with my heartbeat.

"Dude," said Gunner, "that was awesome. You're gonna love the video I got."

Rolling onto my knees, I took some slow breaths while I pulled my helmet and my balaclava off my head. The throb in my head thundered. God, it hurt worse than anything else. It sent off a siren within my ears. I could not hear much of anything for several seconds. I felt dizzy and noticed silvery sparks flying around me like summer fireflies. There was paint from the helmet on the rounded, flat rock. Damn, that hurt. It would've been much worse without my helmet.

"Dude, that looks awful. You want me to get your mom?"

Still unable to talk, I coughed and nodded. He dashed to the house. As my vision stopped blurring, I gasped. The sight shocked me. Something disgusting rested next to the rocks. My mouth dropped open at the sight of some brown and white feathers, a beak and … blood. Holy shit – it's Mr. Owl! What happened? I rushed up to him and examined the carcass. Feathers had scattered while blood and mud had caked the body. I gasped and looked at my helmet, seeing the blood with a few feathers. Oh, no! I killed Mr. Owl. "I'm sorry," I whispered. "I'm so sorry." I let out a long breath, hoping it took away the sadness and guilt.

The chilly wind punched me hard, making it difficult to breathe. Not caring, my shovel hit the ground again, scooped away the wet earth, and threw it into a small pile.

"Jenny," said Uncle Walt, "I'm taking Gunner home. I hope your son is okay. If you're lucky the hit on his head will help him give up those stupid movies Jason used to warp your kids' minds."

Something like an angry spark ignited, mixing with combustible fumes. The explosion pushed out all my feelings into loud, angry words. "Don't you care that your brother died?"

"Your father was a simple-minded fool. I never understood him. We were too different." Uncle Walt's fake sincerity changed to an arrogant rant. "At least I pursued excellence in academia and provided intelligent teaching capacities for people who wish to be enlightened instead of easily amused buffoons who enjoy bottom-feeder movies and television."

"He made a hell of a lot more money than you made!" My blunt, angry voice hoped to hurt him.

Uncle Walt sighed. His thin, gaunt face had a finely trimmed crown of hair. On his chin was an equally kept beard with every whisker shortened evenly. His head lifted high, and his blue eyes looked down smugly. He had a stylish cotton hat, a thin, expensive long coat, and a scarf. I prepared for his usual rant.

"A lot of good it did him," Uncle Walt used his typical pompous tone that irritated all of us. His voice deepened, he enunciated every syllable with precision, and his head lifted higher. "Your father was a continual disappointment and embarrassment to me."

I clutched my shovel tight, wanting to pound him with it. My mouth dropped open when Mom slapped him. He stood shocked holding his cheek where her open palm had struck him.

"Walt," said Mom, "don't ever belittle Jason in front of me or my children again! You are such a selfish, pompous ass. At least Jason tried for years to be close to you, but you refused, always belittling him in your smarmy, arrogant ways. And I know your mother died furious at you for the way you treated him. Your son has a hell of a lot more maturity and wisdom than you do."

Gunner yelped when Uncle Walt grabbed his arm and stormed off. I'll clobber my uncle if he hurts my best friend. I just hope Gunner and I can remain friends. Aunt Beth should slap him as well. More anger flashed when I realized he always referred to Dad as "your father" or "your husband." He could never say, "My brother." I hate him so much.

Mom turned to me. "Honey – hurry up I want to take you to the emergency room." Mom had that stern, concerned look on her face. She was always skinny – too skinny. She had dark hair that tapered off her large forehead riddled with worry lines. Mom said her job was always to worry about me, Elise, and Dad. The wind tried to free her curly dark hair covered by a wool stocking cap. She shoved her hands deep into her thick brown-denim coat pockets. Mom's eyes had a brown tint like mine, but hers were flatter with little to no eyebrows.

I dug some more. "Mom, it's just a stupid bump on the head."

"I don't want to have to bury anyone else anytime soon." Her exasperated voice cracked as she cried.

"Mom," said Elise, "just bury him alive. I'm sure the Earth and worms will spit him back up."

"Shut up!" I snapped.

Mom's voice changed from concern to anger – cutting me. "Young man, we don't say 'shut up' to our relatives – or anyone else for that matter."

I snapped back before Mom could finish her sentence. "She's making jokes when Mr. Owl died, and she's been making snide jokes ever since Dad died and I'm sick of it. She doesn't respect me or my feelings. He was my friend."

"He was a stupid owl," quipped Elise.

With Uncle Walt gone, my rage exploded at Elise. "I thought you were supposed to be the animal rights person of the family! Can't you at least pretend to care? Shit!"

A strong arm pulled me closer. "Let it out," said Father Matthew. He and Sister Regina were visiting with Mom and Elise when Gunner went inside to tell them what happened.

I like him. No – I love him. Maybe he was the uncle I always wanted. Or perhaps a substitute for Dad. Often, I forgot he was a priest. He laughs, tells jokes, talks about how frustrated he gets with God and people. He loves to play chess, and I beat him a couple of times. He would often say a prayer for me before a minibike race started. He could play the guitar and enjoyed playing the blues. He even liked AC/DC, which cracked me up. He didn't pretend to be better than anyone. I didn't understand all of religion, and Catholicism, but Father Matthew made it practical and real. He wanted us to find a way to help people. He wanted the people in his congregation to help at homeless shelters, visit people in the hospital, and give money to the poor box, and he did the same stuff, too. I loved Tuesday nights when I got to help him feed and care for people at the homeless shelter. Since he was blind, I had to help him with the soup ladle. Even if I didn't fully understand all the Bible stories – or even believe some of them – he was a good example to follow.

"Jeffrey," he said, "why don't you finish this burial? Then I can give him the Last Rites and prayer so we can take you to the emergency room." He patted my back and I nodded. I noticed how the wind slightly pushed his reddish blonde hair to the side, framing the tall forehead. His jaw chiseled and tight made him seem like a tough guy, although his genuine smile made him very real. While he wore sunglasses to hide his dilated eyes, I knew they were a strong blue.

I nodded as more tears and snot fell to the already wet ground. Taking a deep breath, I put Mr. Owl's remains into the small grave, then covered the body with the Earth. Mom and Father Matthew stood on either side of me.

"Father Almighty, Maker of Heaven, and Earth, we commit to you our friend, Mr. Owl, to the Earth. Ashes to ashes, dust to dust, as we wait for the final resurrection in the days of when Christ will return and upturn the grave for your glory. Bless this family. Help them grieve for their loss and may they draw closer to you and each other during the trials and tribulations happening at this time. Amen."

We all crossed ourselves. I did kinda like how he pulled me tight like Dad used to. "I'm so sorry about your father. I know it's hard. Mine died when I was young, too."

We walked back towards the house as the frigid wind chapped my lips. "How old were you? What happened?"

"He was a police officer who died in the line of duty. He was shot by a suspect detectives tried to arrest for a murder case. I was 11."

Suddenly, I did not feel so bad. Father Matthew was three years younger than me when he lost his dad. Not that it was fair my dad died, but that would be harder to deal with. "Did you ever hate God for letting your dad die?"

He nodded. "It's perfectly natural and fine to feel that way, too. God's big enough to take it. If you ever want to yell at him – go ahead. It will help you feel better and get it off your chest. I promise you that God won't mind at all. He'd rather you be angry at him than not care or believe in him at all."

"And how old were you when you went blind?"

"I was 21. I've now been blind as long as I could see."

"Did you ever get angry at God for that?"

"Yes," he said quickly, "I did. I yelled at God, I screamed at him, and even swore at him. That helped me get it off my chest. Then once I was done, that's when I heard God."

Is he serious? God speaks to people? For real? "What did God say? What does he sound like?"

He laughed. "You'll probably think I'm crazy, but God talks in subtle ways. It's almost like he talks through your conscience. It's a voice within that's not scary, or angry, or fearful. It's not a voice that makes impressions, says weird things, or makes you question your sanity. But you have to listen and take out those earbuds." No – I didn't have my earbuds in now, but he always talked about how we used our earbuds to block out the world and avoid listening to people and God.

By now we reached Mom's SUV.

Mom and Elise closed their doors while I stood for a second on the running board. "Father Matthew – can you come over for dinner later this week? I have a lot of questions I can't stop thinking about."

"I'd love to," he said. "What about it, Jenny? What night is good for you?"

"Let's try Thursday," Mom suggested. "Anything special you want?"

"The Sister and I would be happy with anything – although your Lemon Chicken would certainly hit the spot." He turned to me. "And Jeffrey, get that head looked at. It's the only one God gave you. Call me if you want to talk. I'll always listen." He patted me on the shoulder. I closed the door, and Mom drove away. I waved at Father Matthew for a split second, forgetting he could not see me wave at him.

I grunted as a spasm of pain shot through my forehead.

From the Inside

"As you can see, the X-Ray shows a definite concussion – and judging by the reports – as of now, it's somewhere between Grade 1 and Grade 2," said Dr. Cox. He was tall, lean, curly haired, and unshaven. He also had a gruff voice that possessed a hint of compassion and care. He turned towards Mom. "Of course, any of the following symptoms could appear within the next four to six days: nausea, headache, dizziness – so keep an eye on him."

The doctor started to put the X-Ray into the folder – but he hesitated and examined it. Pulling it closer to his eyes, and then up to read it through the light.

"Hmm."

"What is it?" asked Mom.

Almost as if drifting to sleep, Dr. Cox did not hear her – at least not immediately. "Oh. Uh, nothing really. The film just had a faint outline. It's probably a little too much exposure or a flaw in the film. "Anyway …

His voice faded as a ringing pierced my ears. Dizziness hit me. My eyes tried to snap shut and I almost fell forward. Elise caught me and pushed me upright. I snapped awake and everyone was around me.

"You alright there, buddy?" asked Dr. Cox.

A sudden headache made me grunt. "I think so."

Mom's quick hands braced my shoulders. Her brown eyes, full of worry, looked at me closely, almost crying. She pushed my bangs back to see me clearly. I knew that look. It was a classic: narrow eyes and wrinkled forehead worked together and finished with her lips pursing. "Sweetie, tell us what's going on."

Dr. Cox put his hand on my shoulder. He shined a light on my eyes again, sweeping the beam to the side. "What's your name?"

"Jeffrey." I answered.

"Where are you?"

"In the hospital?"

"Who's the President?"

I grinned. "Donald Trump – because, you know, the election was rigged and stolen from him."

Dr. Cox laughed. "You had me going there, Jeffrey. I was about to call for the psychiatrist and have you committed to an insane asylum."

"Dr. Cox," said Elise, "Let me test my brother's cognitive abilities with a riddle." She stared at me. "Four cars arrive at an intersection, but they are confused as to who goes first. They all went at the same time, but none of them crashed. How is this possible?"

Despite the pain and ringing, the answer came easily. "They all made right hand-turns."

"Your riddle solving skills qualify you for dork of the year."

The ringing in my head lifted to a higher pitch. "Mom – get Lizzy Borden away from me!"

Elise held up her phone. "Not before I show you the wonderful picture I shot of your butt crack while you were wearing the hospital gown. I think it would make a wonderful Christmas Card."

Mom, angry, seized her phone. "I swear, Elise – stop taking embarrassing pictures of your brother or I'll take that phone away for another month!"

Elise's grin only happened on one side of her face. She was always doing that: taking embarrassing pictures of me – usually in my boxers. One time, she made a video of me singing and dancing in my boxers and uploaded it to YouTube. It got over a million hits before Mom and Dad made her take it down. I got a lot of teasing over that one. Sometimes she'd threaten to send out the picture of me out of the shower to some of her girlfriends – but I had to remind her: *"Sis – you don't have any friends because everyone thinks you're mega-weird."* I sighed, but I could not stay angry at her and showed my own half-smile. "I'm glad to know you're always there to embarrass me, sis. Why do you continuously torture me like this?"

Again, no emotion emanated either from her voice or eyes. "Because I need a hobby that amuses me and belittles you."

The loud ringing erupted, making my head hurt. Flinching, I grunted and dropped my fork.

"Sweetie," Mom said while touching my arm, "what is it? What's wrong?"

My eyelids shut tight for a second. The ringing muffled Mom, Elise, Sister Regina, and Father Matthew. The noise suddenly vanished, as well as the pain. Relieved, I sighed. "I think … I'm okay now."

"Are you sure? Do you want to go back to the hospital?" Worry dripped from her words. "I think we ought to take you back."

"Mom, please." I took a deep breath. "Jeez – who thought a concussion would do this to a guy?"

"Football players, hockey players, boxers, motorcyclists who don't …"

I snapped at Elise. "Shut-up!"

"Jeffrey – don't tell people to 'shut-up.' It's rude and disrespectful," interjected Mom. "How many times do I have to tell you that?"

"You could tell me a thousand times and I'd still tell her to shut-up because she always has that sarcastic tone, making jokes at my expense, and disrespects me. I ask her nicely to be quiet and she continues – so what else am I supposed to do?"

A few tears slipped past Mom's eyes. Her authority vanished. Defeated, her eyes fell into her palm. "Please, kids – stop! I'm tired." Her voice cracked. "We're all mourning the loss of your father. He isn't here anymore to help me." She sighed and remained quiet for a while, until some crying broke the silence. "And I really miss him, too."

A heavy guilt fell on my head – feeling almost like the concussion I got from the minibike accident.

Mom cried for a moment, unable to talk. "I want him back, too." After a few breaths, she composed herself, but I still saw the loneliness in her face. The rich brown color in her eyes faded as tears filled them. Her forehead seemed to multiply the wrinkles. "Please, kids, please. Stop fighting all the time. It wears me out." She took a sip of her wine. She had been drinking more wine lately. It scared me.

Father Matthew quickly embraced Mom. "It's okay, Jenny. Let it out," he whispered. Knowing I should help, my arms wrapped around Mom. She pulled me so tight; I felt her desperation. Elise, who usually hated displays of affection and emotion, reluctantly joined us. We all sat at the table crying as Father Matthew said a prayer. "Father, please comfort this family. Draw them closer to you and each other. Amen."

Theodicy

Father Matthew touched my shoulder as I guided him up the stairs to my room. "Father … why does God let bad things happen?"

He sighed. "That's probably the number one question priests, ministers and Rabbis get asked. It is the one thing people of the cloth get asked more than anything else. And it is the number one thing we all ponder in life. Philosophers, theologians, and laymen have been trying to find the answer for that for many, many centuries." After a slight pause, he grinned lightly, thinking heavily about the question. "In all honesty, I've answered it so much and – well – frankly, even if I could answer that question adequately, I seriously doubt it would help how you or your mother or sister feel."

"Could you try? Because … I really want to know." I helped him to a chair and sat across from him on my bed. Somehow, he looked at me – as a blind person could. His face did not shine, but rather became a little dark. His forehead dropped, and then wrinkled as if he thought hard. I guess that would be the hardest question for anyone, especially a priest, to answer. I wondered if he ever changed his opinion on things like that. And did he doubt God like I've been doing for the last week or so? He rubbed his chin.

"Jeffrey," his smooth, clear voice paused, "terrible things happen to everyone. I've gone blind. You lost your father. I've lost my father. Others have lost their lives to disease or war, or just part of their bodies. Some women die in childbirth. Sadly, suffering is part of life. We want it removed from our lives through all kinds of means like money, health, hobbies, or family. But no one is immune from pain and suffering.

"Ironically, that is what makes us stronger eventually. Like an athlete who runs more, they feel pain, but it makes them stronger. Lifting weights stops doing good when we do not push ourselves beyond our current abilities. Have you ever felt a burning when lifting weights?"

"Yes, sir."

"That pain is your muscles being torn down and rebuilding new muscle that makes you stronger. If we had a life free of pain and suffering, we would not grow stronger physically, emotionally, and spiritually. Like a parent, God wants us to mature and become stronger. That would not happen if there was no pain or suffering.

And he does take a huge risk in letting terrible things happen. Will that drive someone away from him, or closer to him?

"Also, we are free spirits. God wants us to love him – but he doesn't want us programmed to love. He does not want robots who worship him without free will. If we did operate like that, we would not respond to him out of real love.

"And with free will comes a price: decisions to drive drunk, or perhaps become so angry that someone lashes out in revenge. Many fellow priests have abused children and caused so much pain and suffering I cannot fathom. And to assume God will provide relief for the victims in this world is a way of assuming we bear no response of our own. When we see injustice, and suffering, God calls us to do something about it that reveals his grace and love. We are his hands and feet to dispense that grace.

"Like I said – there are no easy answers and we've been trying to figure this out for centuries. All you can do is not let this pain drive you away from God but draw closer to him. That means a lot of prayer, tears, and fellowship to deal with that pain. I know this is an extremely hard and bitter pill to swallow – especially at your age." He hesitated for several seconds. "I hope you understand."

I sighed. "You're right. It doesn't make me feel any better. I guess you should ask for your money back from the seminary."

He laughed subtly, letting it come in short, skipping chuckles. "I love talking with you. I love your honesty."

I smiled. He hugged me with one arm. "If you ever want to talk to me about anything, please call me. I may not have the best answers – but I'll always listen. Do the same if you're worried about your mother or sister. I'm here for you. Do you want me to pray with you?"

After a few seconds of thinking, I shook my head – then remembered he couldn't see me do that. "I think I need to figure out my own prayers."

He nodded. "You're right. But if you want me to help, let me know." He stood, so I led him back downstairs to the living room where Sister Regina spoke with Mom and Elise. "Sister, I think it's time to return to the parsonage."

After a few exchanges of "good-byes" and "thank-yous," the door closed, and they left.

An eerie silence froze me. Glancing around, examining every corner, I tried to find something – although I did not know what it could be. I felt a tense shakiness just underneath my skin. Cold pricks pressed from within, causing my lips to quiver and my breaths to quicken. Something watched me. It felt creepy, uneasy, and frightening. The unseen eyes cast cold and sharp blades at me, as if they wanted to harm me. Was this real – or am I just being paranoid?

Afraid to turn off the light at the entry door, I left it on, backing up as I searched. Nothing. It sure seemed like something was there, stalking me, watching every move, as if waiting for the right moment to strike.

Hell is Living Without You

The piano music sounded soothing. I recognized it instantly: "Home Sweet Home," by Motley Crue. It was Mom's favorite song. I stood just beyond the arch to the piano room, listening. She could play a lot of songs on the piano: "Come Sail Away" and "Lady" by Styx, "Beth" by KISS, and so many others. She liked to joke that her mind clung to the memories of 1970s and 1980s classic rock and metal – and that's what kept her young-looking. When her music came on, the volume went up and she smiled.

Everyone said Mom and Dad were made for each other. Their first date was a Motley Crue concert. They lived for heavy metal music of the 1980s, concerts, horror movies, baseball, and football. Mom and Dad's favorite musician was Alice Cooper and even forced Elise and me to attend his concerts. Well, after the first couple, they didn't force me to see him because his music really grew on me. Elise liked his concerts, too. They fit her mood and personality.

I peered around the door with one eye as the music subsided, ebbing away. She wasn't smiling. Her eyes had a darker color and her mouth frowned, making it easier for tears to stream down her cheeks. As I recalled how silly they acted together, I smiled. It faded thinking of Dad being gone.

The vibration of the last few notes still hung in the air, but they slowly faded into nothing, stilling the air. Mom leaned forward, placing her arms on the top of the piano. They cradled her chin as she stared at the picture. I could tell it was the one of Dad. Next to it was the poetry box. A few of the poems Dad wrote her rested on the piano top. She had put a lot of them to music she created. She always said, *"My heart and soul instinctively tell my hands to play. My fingers don't know which note I'll hit first ... or last."*

Mom lifted her head. Her mouth moved, saying nothing and something at the same time. I easily read her lips. "I miss you so much." She sipped her almost empty wine glass. I retreated as her eyes pivoted towards me.

I keep forgetting she lost her husband. To me, it seemed like I was the one who lost the most, but Mom was married for five years before Elise and I were born. I wonder how she felt. Was it a deeper pain than what I experienced? Or was it so different I could not understand

it? I know Mom lost her baby brother a long time ago –
and he was only 10 or so.

For the first time, I cried for Mom and her pain. Now,
I was confused. What should I do? I let out a long sigh.

*"When we see injustice, and suffering, God calls us to
do something about it that reveals his grace and love. We
are his hands and feet to dispense that grace."*

Father Matthew's words, etched in my memory,
prompted me. Leaning against the wall, I wondered what
her emptiness felt like. Should I comfort her some more?
She was all I had left as a parent. With Elise being so
unemotional and cynical, I guess it was up to me to help
Mom.

Startled, she tried to straighten up herself. She dried
her tears, put the poems back in the box and forced a
smile. "Hi, sweetie," she said, "I was just …"

"I'm sorry you lost your husband," I whispered. "And
your baby brother."

Mom's arms, although skinny, squeezed tightly.

"Father Matthew told me to let it all out. You need to
do that, too. Please, Mom. Let it all out."

Her warm tears pushed through my shirt and onto my
shoulders as the sobs rushed uncontrollably. She
bellowed for two, three … maybe even five minutes.
After she purged the depression, Mom took in several

sighs. Her fingers swiped away the remaining tears. Still sitting on the piano bench, she stared at me. Mom's face, pale, desperate, somehow managed a weak smile. "Thank-you so much for being here for me. I don't know what I'd do without you, sweetie. I love you and your sister so much."

Bad Place Alone

I reluctantly gave Mom my smart phone. She said the blue light tricked my brain to think it was day and hindered sleep. Every night I wondered if that was true or not. I kept forgetting to look that up on Google. Uncle Walt and Aunt Beth took Gunner's phone, too.

My friends, Tucker, and Chuck, though, could have their phones in bed with them – and stayed up late chatting, texting, and doing facetime. I guess that would keep me from sleeping. Also, they did fall asleep in school a lot.

Mom also took Elise's phone as well – but she did not have friends. She spooked most of her peers away – even the ones that were sort of like her. I guess she might be looking stuff up on her phone until late, and perhaps trolling social media.

Turning off the lights, I crawled into bed and turned on my side. Freddy jumped into the bed and curled in a ball near my legs. Reaching towards him, I pet him. Freddy licked my hand. It tickled me, which made me smile. I heard him yawn. "Good night, Freddy," I whispered.

I kept thinking about what Father Matthew told me about evil and suffering. I was unsure about his explanation, and lately been more unsure that God existed. Elise said she didn't believe in God, but she's the kind of person who would tell a bunch of Atheists that she did believe in God … and that she (and God) did not believe in them. I let loose a half-smile thinking about her.

My eyes had adjusted to the dark. Noticing the picture of me and Dad at the Pittsburgh Pirates baseball game, I smiled thinking about him. I could see his big brown eyes that laughed with his wide smile. His laughter always came from his belly – much as I imagined what Santa Claus would be like (if there was a Santa). Dad did have a thick, brown beard that had many specks of grey, but he had a decent amount of hair on top of his head. I hope I don't dream about him. It hurts when I wake up and he's not around.

I smiled more, thinking how Dad got me into horror movies – both from the 1980s back to the classics like "Frankenstein, "Dracula" to modern horror like "Insidious" and "The Conjuring" universe. In fact, his name was Jason Michael – although he was born about five years before the "Friday the 13th" and "Halloween" movies. Also, I always thought it was funny he was born on Halloween. He got all the jokes when in middle and high school. "Whenever people saw me, they'd go 'chi chi chi, ka ka ka.'" Of course, that was in a week when a month got a Friday the 13th. Near Halloween, people called him Michael and would mimic the Halloween soundtrack. Dad's voice had etched strongly in my memories.

My eyelids became heavy. A gentle whisper found my ears. I couldn't understand it. Yawning, sleep draped over me like a blanket. As my eyes closed, the whispers grew a bit louder. It got cold, making my teeth chatter. I shivered under the covers. A few images repeated in my head, fast as if I kept changing from three channels. The first image was Dad alive. The next one was his coffin lowered to the ground. The third one was something … hideous and dark. The images repeated. What is that thing? The shadowy one. Its unproportioned arms and sinewy legs forced it to hunch. Its eyes glowed a subtle red. The shoulders spiked. Dark wings spread. The cold returned with force, slapping my skin. Whenever it appeared, my stomach knotted. The knot carried a terror that spread into my body: the arms, the legs, the mid-core region, and my head. The fear became a cold dread, similar to when I fell through some ice into the river when I was ten. The shocking cold wrapped around me from head to toe. The freezing cold enveloped me and I panicked. Dad and Mom saved me. It was the most frightening moment in my life. I hated that memory.

A better memory surfaced: Dad and I worked on my minibike engine. "We're gonna make this work because I love you and want you to win this race." He smiled when I looked at him. His long beard could never hide that smile. Although he had a gut, it was not big. His laugh was friendly and comforting. I felt warm – especially inside my chest and stomach.

Standing close to the window, the monster blotted out what light the moon provided. Unable to see the face, I sat up in bed. The terror and dread returned – making me want to run away. Frozen in bed, I pulled my blankets tight – partly for protection and partly for warmth. However, the chill broke through my flannel comforter. Also, what was that smell? It reminded me of the rotting meat Dad and I found while hiking at Mount Bigelow. We guessed a bear, or a mountain lion had mangled a big deer. Maggots were squirming, flies buzzing, adding to the mega disgusting stench. I almost threw up.

Scared, I somehow remembered the prayer Father Matthew taught me. I recited it – not just in my head but also with my mouth, saying it aloud. "O Lord my God, be not far from me. O my God, hasten to help me, for varied thoughts and great fears have risen within me, afflicting my soul. How shall I escape them unharmed? How shall I dispel them?

"I will go before you," says the Lord, "and will humble the great ones of earth. I will open the doors of the prison and will reveal to you hidden secrets."

"Do as You say, Lord, and let all evil thoughts fly from Your face. This is my hope and my only comfort— to fly to You in all tribulation, to confide in You, and to call on You from the depths of my heart and await patiently for Your consolation."

The terror slowly faded. I fell asleep.

Mr. Owl? I thought he was dead. He looked at me from the rafters – although his eyes appeared larger than normal. Strange shadows stretched across the walls, and the high ceiling. The shed appeared wider, too. Walls seemed to be missing and replaced with dark and cold shadows.

Mr. Owl's yellowish eyes grew larger, then the inside lids sloped down towards his beak – making him look sinister. He glared at me while the yellowish color intensified. His beak opened wide.

The image changed. Dad. He smiled at me. How was he back? Confused, I accepted it. His dirty hands pushed my hair back, then he hugged me. I grabbed him tightly, never wanting to let go. "I miss you, Dad. I miss you so much."

"I miss you, too, boy. Son."

The embrace turned cold. A wave of dread splashed over me. My heart raced. My skin, hands, and feet all shook. I tried to pull away, but Dad – or rather something with sinewy arms – pulled me tighter. Unable to breathe, I kicked and screamed. I looked up to beg him to let go. I saw it!

It had a thin cadaverous head. The eyes, humongous, were deep empty sockets. Pieces of flesh peeled away. A huge set of fangs jutted down from the top jaw. The cavernous mouth hissed at me. Its putrid breath made me gag. I tried to pull away as it pulled me closer. Its fangs grew longer as it lifted its head higher. The sharp teeth jabbed into the back of my shoulder. A vicious pain spread through my skin and burrowed into my muscles, bones, and my soul. The pain spread across my back, forcing my shoulders to cringe. Now the dull pain shot through my arms, into my hands and fingers.

I woke up to Freddy barking. He growled slightly. He jumped off the bed and pushed the slightly ajar door open with his snout.

My breath raged out of control. Clutching my chest, I hoped to calm my lungs, my heart, and my stomach. Sweat poured heavily, drenching my skin in the freezing air. Inhaling deeply for a minute or two, my respiration and heartbeat slowed, matching in perfect rhythm. The sweating ceased.

A shadow blocked the moonlight. Turning, my soul tried to jump free from my body, producing a jerk. It stopped immediately as a smile broke across my face. I recognized the silhouette that also revealed the beard. "I miss you, Dad."

He reached down and touched my forehead. Instantly the serenity vanished as a cold icicle protruded through my head, into my neck, down my chest and through my body. An icy mist fell from his mouth that now hung agape with saliva dripping a horrid smell that fell on my face. His fingers, cold, long, and stretched, stroked my hair. Terror seized my body, making it impossible to move, as if I froze to the bed. The hideous eyes, black and sunken, hid below a large, misshapen forehead.

"Relax, son," he said gently.

Despite the horror, I managed to speak. "You're not my dad!"

For a second, the thing took the appearance of my father. "Please let me stay, son. I want to be with you forever."

I found new tears. The first kind were the ones pushed out by sorrow, sadness, pain, and regret that made a body sob in desperation. The second type, the warm ones, did not drown me in uncontrollable bellowing, but rather weep warm, comforting tears of healing and joy. This new type, though, had a bitter coldness like an icy river that made my skin cringe and paralyzed my thoughts, emotions, and body. Horrific fear pushed them out.

"You're not my dad!"

The thing stood a massive height over me. Its wings spread wide, hiding its ugliness in shadow, but circulating the dead air and vile smell. Its bellowing crushed my ears, drowning my painful screams.

No More Mr. Nice Guy

My shaking hands turned on the shower water. The warm spray exploded and circled the stand-alone tub. I closed the shower curtain and adjusted the temperature. Yes – it did help. The hot waters fell down my chest, arms, and legs and pushed away my anxiety. The coldness just underneath my skin vanished. As I let out a huge breath – the lingering uneasiness left.

I turned, then cringed as a stinging pain shot across my back. Wherever the spray landed, the burning sting sent out an explosion of pain that spread like wildfire. My eyes and teeth clenched, I pivoted to face the spray so I could bear it. Huffing, I counted the seconds until the pain dissipated. "Shit, shit, shit, shit, shit …" I must have said it ten or twelve times. Was it that that made the pain go away – or was it the grunts that came between them?

Somehow, I got clean (at least my front). After the water stopped, I stepped on the aging bathmat and grabbed a towel. Trying to dry my back, the pain exploded again. While some of it was like a stinging fire, others were like a numbing, dull pain. I dropped the towel and leaned against the white porcelain sink, cringing from the agony. I yelled. "Sis. Sis! Help!" I didn't care that I was naked. The mega-pain almost made me cry.

"Oh, Holy Mother Mary May I!" Elise's voice usually had no emotion, but now it brimmed with terror. That was the only time she ever uttered her favorite phrase of shock. She said it again – a little softer. "Holy Mother Mary May I." It faded into nothing.

"Stand still," she said. "I'll dry you." She patted my back gently – which still sent a barrage of vicious aches everywhere in my torso. It felt like a tsunami slapping onto a shoreline. Every spike of soreness followed, forcing me to clench my teeth, grunt, and huff out a breath. Every surge diminished in power until the waves returned to normal surf breaking on the beach.

Sis handed me the towel and rushed out while I dried my front and put on some boxer shorts. Before I could pull them on fully, I heard the click of a smartphone. "What the hell, Elise? Stop taking …"

She shoved the phone in front of me and I saw it. My mouth hung open at the sight. I grabbed the phone to get a closer look. On the top of my right shoulder, some sort of scar raked across my back almost to my left shoulder blade. Two more, slightly staggered and below the first one, also stretched from one side to the other. My lower back had three darkened bruises. The images shuddered my breathing, my thinking, and my soul. My mind clicked back on and tried to think of anything that could have led to such injuries. The mini-bike crash? No. Surely, Dr. Cox would have noticed it when examining me.

"How did that happen?" For a change, Elise's voice and eyes had some genuine caring. "I didn't see any of this yesterday at the Emergency Room." Her eyes instantly returned to their regular emotionless state – as well as her voice. "You're becoming a zombie. I just know it. You move slow, you make grunting noises, and you have minimal brain function."

"Come on, Sis. Give me a break." I kept looking at the picture. "What could possibly explain this?"

After drying and getting my pants on, I showed the bruises and scars to Mom. Perplexed, she kept pushing me to stay home from school today. No. I couldn't believe I preferred school to staying home. I had been in the house grieving all last week. I wanted to be around other people – even if most of my demented classmates had no soul, no intelligence, and no thought. Oh, no! I'm becoming like Elise!

The pain faded after some ibuprofen, some skin cream medication, and a few bandages. The anxiety returned, though. Uneasy, afraid, my hands started shaking. It was like a cold buzz just underneath my skin. It spread like tiny ants crawling inside, circling my heart, and multiplying to other parts of my body – even my dick. That's mega-weird.

"What's wrong with you?" Mom asked.

"I don't know. I had a real creepy dream last night." The tension did not go away. I tried the prayer again for the tenth or twelfth time. I lost count of how many times I crossed myself. The prayer worked, but every time, the calming effect faded faster.

I sighed, hoping I could find some normalcy again.

We got our school pictures today. Although my fingers still shook, I managed to get the photos out of the envelope. I took a quick glance and started to hide my pictures before anyone could ask to see them. For some reason, I stopped and examined it. No longer fearful of my image, I finally liked it. The little layer of fat I had disappeared and now I had a jawline and a lean chin. My teeth, no longer with braces, showed between my lips that had thinned over the last year. My brown eyes had also become sleek, although my eyebrows remained thick. My hair, parted in the middle, was long even with a few bangs stringing over my eyes. Content with my image for the first time, I smiled, reflecting on the picture. I still wished I'd get that growth spurt Mom and Dad always talked about. I'm only five feet and two inches tall.

"You look dorky," Elise quipped.

Why did they put us in the same biology and English classes together? I had to put up with her at home – but now also two classes in school? Sheesh. I mean, I love her like my sister – but we needed a break from each other. I'll bet she even bugged me when we were together in Mom's womb.

"And you look mega retarded." She poked me hard with her elbow. "Ow," I said. "Knock it off, Lizzy Borden."

"Do you two have a problem?" asked Mr. Sumner.

"No, sir," we both said. He was a mean teacher. Mr. Sumner could teach, but he was strict and didn't like putting up with any nonsense in his class. I guess trying to teach 20 or so freshmen would piss off anyone. At least Mr. Sumner seemed a little more compassionate today. He suggested Elise and I write about Dad, what he was like and what we missed about him. I was eager to try it. I kinda liked writing. It sounded like a good way to communicate how I feel.

"Can I just write an essay about why I hate everyone in this school and wish I could watch them as they all got sick with the Bubonic Plague and slowly rot into a bag of bones while rats feed on their dead bodies?"

Mr. Sumner rolled his eyes at Elise and then shook his head.

The bell rang. Freedom. At least for five minutes – and I could get away from Elise. She could be so annoying. Of course, she just didn't annoy me. Her skills at irking people crossed ethnic lines, gender lines, socio-economic statuses, and age lines, pissing off boys, girls, teachers, principals, parents, and I think she even irritated animals.

Uh, oh. Casey Righetti stormed toward Elise, and he looked pissed. I better go and try and stop him from being a jerk and picking on her. Or was I saving him from Elise's annoying personality?

"Hey, you psychopathic weirdo," he said. Casey's voice carried. It reminded me of that Eric Cartman cartoon character Dad thought was hilarious. It was the type of voice that tried to sound tougher than it really was and came off as phony. "I heard you've been calling me names behind my back," he said.

Elise, unfazed, looked at him ambivalently through her oversized, round glasses. "Oh. Would you rather I say them to your face? Okay. Ignoramus. Dolt. Sasquatch. Idiot. How about a Shakespearean insult? Pugnacious Puss-filled Pewter …"

A fury ignited inside me as Casey shoved her. "Hey, you fucking ass-wipe! You don't push a girl – especially my sister!"

"And what are you going to do about it, asshole?" With the last word, he shoved me back a few steps. The crowd that gathered had their phones out, anticipating a video to upload to YouTube. I took a few steps forward. I squinted as that annoying ringing erupted in my ears. It added to my simmering rage that spread like a fire – erupting from my heart into every bone, muscle, and limb.

"Try anything, asshole, and I'll make you wish you killed yourself – just like your dad. I'll bet he did that because he's embarrassed by the two of ..."

The rage exploded as lights dimmed into a red haze that darkened more. I'm not too sure how long it lasted, but the fury erased the world around me. Finding independence from my anger, I returned to reality. On top of Casey, I had pounded his face, although I'm not too sure how many times. His eyes were watering, his nose bled, and swelled just like his lip. At that point, someone jerked me off him. Massive, strong arms wrapped around me. Another surge of anger exploded, helping me break from the captor's arms. Something in me snickered and laughed. It goaded me to finish the job and beat him to a bloody pulp – even though I already hurt him.

What's wrong with me? I've never been in a fight before, nor have I wanted to hurt someone so badly, and never hated anyone so much.

Fortunately, the person who seized me earlier grabbed me again and squeezed tighter. Unable to move my arms, I kicked and screamed. "Let go of me you asshole! Let go of me or I'll fucking kill you! I'll fucking …" My foot found one of his kneecaps, and he groaned. My arms weakened his massive grip over my chest and shoulders, but he kept the hold while grunting. My anger suddenly vanished as the ringing in my head faltered. After a huge sigh, he set me down.

It was Mr. Hamilton! He ran the in-school detention section. He was a huge, strong black man who used to run the intake center for juvenile delinquents in the county. I broke free from his grip? No way. He had huge muscles and played linebacker for the Buffalo Bills for three years before returning to Newcastle to be an educator and help reform troubled kids.

Shocked, silent, all the students took a few steps back. Scared, they all let out a huge breath and backed away more once Mr. Hamilton released me. Even Elise seemed overwhelmed by my vicious anger. They all quivered, staring at me as if they were terrified. Immediately, the school security officer cuffed my hands behind my back while the nurse arrived and rendered first aid.

Shocked, I cried looking at Casey's bloodied and bruised head. Why would I do that? I felt the warm blood on my knuckles and noticed some of it was on my face and clothes. Oh, shit! I'm in mega trouble!

Mom watched the video Elise got of me attacking Casey. She cringed and covered her mouth – although I wasn't sure if it was because of the violence, or the horrible things I did not remember saying. After the video, she glared at me, tilting her head to the left. The vein in her forehead throbbed. Maybe this is why I kept my bangs a little long. Sure, they were fine when I parted my hair in the middle – but when I looked down from Mom, they fell just a bit over my eyes. That gave me a shield when she or Dad were upset with me. I glanced at her subtly, barely making eye contact with Mom who didn't move a muscle. Was she going to stare at me until my whole body froze? Her glazed eyes pierced me like needles, knives, and swords. Terrified, I gasped, hoping the stare would not destroy me.

The principal, Mr. Clayton, talked to her. "I know this isn't easy – especially after your tragic loss. But … per regulations and policy, I have to suspend Jeffrey for the remainder of the school year. He'll have to do distance learning – which means getting his assignments online and turning them into his teachers. He'll have to email them or leave voicemails. After such an assault, we cannot even have him as an in-school suspension."

"I understand," Mom said quietly – finally looking at Mr. Clayton. "I am very, very sorry about this whole ordeal." Her words were quick, sharp, and blunt. "He'll receive adequate punishment at home."

"And Mrs. McPherson, I don't know what Mr. and Mrs. Righetti are considering – but one of their options is to file assault charges against Jeffrey – so he could face criminal prosecution. Or they could file a Civil Suit against you. Either way, you may want to talk to a lawyer."

Standing, I protested loudly. "He pushed my sister. He pushed me. What am I supposed to do?"

Mr. Clayton sighed and gave me the "disappointed" look Dad often used. It jabbed a stick into an already painful wound. It hurt more than those bruises on my back.

"Jeffrey, I can understand you standing up for yourself and your sister. If you had thrown one or two punches, I could put you in in-school suspension. But your attack was so violent … I have no other options. And I know you've been through a terrible loss. I cannot imagine the pain of losing your father at such a young age. But you're the man of the house, now. I know it's a huge responsibility thrown at you abruptly, but you can't afford to act like that. You also injured Mr. Hamilton. Do you understand the seriousness of the situation?"

I nodded while wiping some tears. "Yes, sir."

Gathering my books, papers, and laptop, I cringed at the thought of distance learning. I had to endure that shit a few years ago when Covid was rampant. Now I gotta do it again? What the fuck was I thinking? I'm mega stupid.

The car ride home was so quiet. Elise and I never put in our earbuds. Mom stared straight ahead and remained quiet as we drove through town. The gray skies and intermittent rain added to the cold emptiness we all shared. Stopped at a red light, Mom closed her eyes, covered her face, and cried.

The light changed to green. Mom never noticed, until a car behind us honked. Pulled back to reality, she made the first turn into a parking lot and stopped. She reached for the tissue paper and dried her eyes.

It was all my fault. Ashamed, I dropped my head and found the familiar and painful sadness. "I'm sorry,

Mom." I hope she understood me. "I really am. I don't know what I was thinking."

Mom pulled me closer and hugged me tightly. After a minute or so, she backed away and looked at me intently. Brushing my hair out of my eyes, she then cradled my jaw with her hands. "I love you – but none of us need this right now. Mr. Clayton is right: you're the man of the house, now. I really need you to think before you act – especially in these situations. If you face civil or criminal charges, I might have to get a lawyer and they're expensive. Do you understand me? You could end up in a juvenile detention center with violent boys for … six months … a year … or God knows how much time. Do you understand that? Do you understand how badly you hurt that boy? Do you understand the trouble you're in? Do you understand I'll have to pay the medical bills? And now lawyer fees." Her whole face cringed.

I nodded as best as I could with my jaw in her hand. I sniffed. She gave me some tissues. After drying my eyes and cheeks, I blew my nose. Suddenly the possibility of spending time in a prison with a bunch of tough jerks made my heart freeze. What if they … I didn't want to think about that.

"I'll be here for you and Elise," Mom whispered, "but I also need you to be here for us, too. Okay?"

I nodded. "Okay, Mom. I will."

What Do You Want from Me?

My whole body sobbed. My eyes, nose, mouth, and chest all worked together to expel the sadness and fear. I haven't been able to talk for the last several minutes.

"Jeffrey, just let it all out."

I did not detect any judgment, disappointment, or anger in Father Matthew's voice. Yet, I could not help feeling so bad – like there was nothing good in me. Taking a huge breath, and a second one, I kept the emotions at bay for a split second. "I've hurt everyone: Casey, his parents, Mom, and myself. Why'd I do that?" The dark confessional booth seemed to make things worse. "I don't know what to do. I'm mega scared."

"Jeffrey," he paused a moment, "I want you to understand something: you will make mistakes, errors in judgment, and sins. And when I see you upset over those things, I know your heart is repenting. That is the first step in forgiveness."

I remained quiet for a minute. "But will Mom forgive me? What about Casey and his mom?"

"Jeffrey, understand that Moses needed forgiveness. He killed an Egyptian. Peter needed forgiveness for denying Jesus three times. St. Augustine needed forgiveness, as well as Martin Luther."

It was hard to relate my life right now with those people because they were in history – so far removed from me. My emotions retreated and gave me rest. I sighed. Able to think, Father Matthew's words gently found their way into my heart. The guilt weakened. It retreated until a small spark ignited and brought some warmth. "So, what do I have to do?"

"First, pray. Next, seek forgiveness from those you have wronged: your mom, Casey, and the man who you kicked in the knees. Perhaps your principal, too."

"How?"

"Start by writing a letter. Why don't you write them, then bring them back to me. I'll read them and give you some feedback."

I crossed myself. "Thank-you, Father." He said a prayer.

I exited the confessional booth. He came out, too, and we faced each other. I wrapped my arms around him and squeezed as tight as I could. As he reciprocated, it felt familiar – but not quite the same as Dad's hugs. Still, anxiety and fear retreated, and guilt either hid or ran away. "Thank-you, Father."

He patted my back. "Anytime, Jeffrey."

Mom stood behind me, clasping both my shoulders and rubbing them. "Thank-you, Father. He insisted on seeing you."

"It's always my pleasure to help anyone in my parish – especially those going through tough times and pain. I am also looking forward to dinner tomorrow night. What time do you want me and Sister Regina to come over?"

"Maybe 6:30 or so."

"I can't wait."

Something whispered in my ear. What did it say? I concentrated. My eyes flinched when the ringing returned. Did the voice say something else?

"Did you guys hear that?"

"What, sweetie?" Mom said while stroking my hair. "Did we hear what?"

I thought about it. It sorta sounded like Dad. Or was the voice there? Unsure, I tried to listen intently. Not hearing anything, I hunched my shoulders. "I'm not sure." Trying to remember the voice, and finding it seemed elusive. I hunched my shoulders. "I guess it was nothing."

Come Inside

A stinging pain irritated my eyes as I opened them. Although the room was dark, I found it difficult to keep them open. However, I heard three loud bangs on the door. After a few seconds, three more resounded. Pushing the covers off, I lay there for a minute as the pounding continued – somehow calling out to me. Exhausted, I sat up, wishing Mom would get the door – or maybe Elise could.

I cursed and stood. Somehow the cold embedded in the wooden floor pushed through my wool socks. It continued to spread to my soles, up my ankles and shins to my knees. "Alright – I'm coming," I yelled at the continuous knocking. My shoulder slapped the door frame as I stepped onto the second-floor landing. I had to use the handrail to guide me downstairs since those lights didn't work, either.

Now the knocking noise was overbearing. Using my hands, I found the deadbolt, turned it, and pulled the door in. Dead chilly air rushed inside, squeezing my shoulders, arms, and chest. I wanted to pull away, but something invisible held me. The porch light did not work. There did not seem to be any light from the moon or stars, either.

A face emerged – casting its own illumination. The friendly brown eyes, the smile, the long beard that had streaks of gray in them. I smiled. "Dad." He wore a Metallica T-shirt under his unbuttoned blue flannel shirt. His big arms wrapped around me. He smelled of sweat – as if working on engines. I sighed recognizing the annoying, yet familiar scent. I whispered, "Dad – I want you back so bad. It hurts so much that you're not here. My life is falling apart. Please come back."

"Let me in, son. I can make all the bad feelings go away. Trust me."

Unable to resist, I grabbed him. I wanted to pull him as tight as I could and relish the warmth and comfort.

My tears dried. Love disappeared as a bubbling fear swelled. Warmth switched to bitter cold, and hope turned into dread as the door slammed. Where'd Dad go? The house became quiet. Darkness encroached – first making the door, the windows, and the furniture disappear. It sounded like a crackling as the cold shadows closed in and trapped me. Freezing, I tried to warm my arms and torso while retreating. "Dad? Dad?" My voice echoed as if in a large house – or more like an empty garage. "Dad? Where are you? Dad? Help."

The darkness, about to swallow me, forced one more scream. "Dad!"

**This House is Haunted**

"That sounds like some dream," Mom said before a sip of coffee. "It helps to talk about those things and get them off your mind."

"It was really creepy." I still shuddered from the dream.

"You've been having a lot of bad dreams," she said while pushing my bangs back. "Are you sure you don't need to see a counselor? More than Father Matthew?"

"I dunno."

"He's going crazy," said Elise. "He has all the symptoms: bad dreams, crying, beating the shit out of people, and short appendages unique to the male species."

"Elise, sh …" I glanced at Mom, and somehow stopped myself. "Elise, quit being a mega-bitch."

Mom shook her head, dropped her face to her palm, and sighed. "At least you didn't tell her to 'shut up.'"

I kinda smiled at that one. It alleviated another issue facing me today: talking with attorneys and the Righetti's. I thought it might take longer, say a month or so. However, it was only a little more than a week. They had a personal lawyer and a county prosecutor.

We had our Lawyer, too: Mrs. Regur. She was an old family friend and one of the smartest women I ever knew. She let me call her Lillian.

"How are you doing, kiddo?" She tussled my hair – which always made me grin. "The more you grow up, the more handsome you get." Lillian was a little hefty but had boundless energy and a passion for being a family lawyer. She had short, curly-brown hair and wore thick glasses that made her look mega smart. She also goes to St. Patrick's Cathedral with us where Father Matthew is the Priest.

Lillian sat at the breakfast table as Mom and I listened intently. "Now I've already talked to them, myself. What they are asking for is compensation for the surgery he's going to need, as well as the medical bills, and they wanted another 50 percent for pain and suffering, but state law prevents the latter. The tort can only be a maximum of 20 percent. I might be able to talk them down to ten percent. However, I need to know that you are remorseful for what you did. That means you're sorry."

Even though I knew what 'remorseful' meant, I nodded. "I went to church and confessed to Father Matthew."

"I'm glad to hear that."

"Lillian," my voice faded as uncertainty darkened my eyes. "Is there a chance I will go to a jail for kids?"

She smiled and shook her head. "No, honey. It's your first offense. Typically, in a case like this, even if you went to court, you'd get a year's probation and a suspended sentence."

"What's that mean?"

"You have to be on your best behavior for a year – maybe just six months. If you got into another fight either with this boy – or another – then you could get six to twelve months in a Juvenile Detention Center."

I felt my heart relax. No longer taut or frozen, it allowed me to breathe normally and push the fear out of my mind. I hugged her. "Thank-you. I was scared of being put in a jail for kids."

She smiled. "Now can you be polite and respectful to the lawyers you're about to talk to?"

I nodded. "Yes ma'am"

"Good. We need to get going soon. So, get ready."

My stomach knotted. I licked my lips and blew out my breath. I had to dress nicely – even wear a tie. Mom had to help me with it.

"You know how important this is, right?" Mom asked.

Afraid to talk, I simply nodded. Mom looked very worried. One tear leaked from the inside corner of her left eye. The prominent brown color deepened. Her face wrinkled on itself. She curled her lips. Mom kissed my forehead. "Okay," she whispered. "Let's go."

Elise had to ride the bus to school. Mom knew it was best to keep us separated before such a big meeting. I thought so, too – and even Sis knew it was best. I did not need anyone agitating me before talking to a bunch of lawyers.

The offices were nice: richly decorated with nice pictures, thick red carpeting, and large desks. Was that meant to scare me or other people when talking with lawyers? Or was it just to show off?

My stomach knotted tighter. I hoped I didn't do anything that would blow apart the deal. We had a short wait in the lobby, then a lady escorted us to a private office. My knees shook, my shoulders tightened, and pools of sweat drenched my hands. Guilt flushed through my mind for what I did to Casey – and for putting Mom in such a horrible situation.

The long, torturous wait ended as Casey and his parents walked in – along with two other men. One sat behind the desk, the other next to him. Wishing I could hide from Casey and his parents' eyes, I looked down at the carpet. No, I should face him to see what I did. Casey's face was still swollen and had cuts and gashes. I suddenly felt awful about what I did.

Lillian shook hands with Mr. and Mrs. Righetti's attorney.

"Mrs. McPherson, Jeffrey, Lillian, thank-you for joining us," said the man behind the desk. I examined him: stout, heavy in the middle, with a bald head and a thick goatee. I glanced at his name plate: Richard Dumas. I almost laughed imagining Elise being here and responding, *"Thank-you, Mr. Dumbass."* Somehow, I stifled my amusement.

"Good morning," said Mom.

She poked me. I stood and reached to shake his hand. Damn, his grip hurt. "Uh, good morning, sir."

I glanced over at the other man. "I'm George Winter, and I'm the district attorney assigned to this case." He was much thinner and neater, not having any facial hair at all. He smiled and shook Mom's hand. I wasn't sure if I had to – but once he offered, I knew it would be better if I did. His grip, too, was so strong it almost hurt.

Should I apologize to Casey and his parents? I shot a couple of quick glances. "Um … Casey." Nervous, I stuttered. "I'm really sorry I beat you up."

His mom leaned towards me. She was a large woman – not fat, but husky, tall, and her voice was lower than most women. "You little bastard! My son won't have the full function of his left eye possibly for the rest of his life. You knocked a tooth out!"

Scared, I jumped back. I cried slightly and looked down at the carpet.

"Donna," said Mr. Dumas, "I told you to keep calm. He is apologizing, which is something you wanted. Let George and I take …" He couldn't finish.

"You two wanna play nice," she said, "but I don't. You want leniency, and possible restitution." Mrs. Righetti's husband tried to take her hand and sit her down, but she pulled her arm from him. She turned towards Mom. "And what kind of monster are you raising, Jenny? He's psychotic. It's all those horror movies you and Jason let him watch. I – "

My nervous heartbeat changed. It pounded like heavy footsteps of someone in a rage. I kept hearing whispers growing louder, echoing like voices in a cavern or a canyon. They tickled my ears – but not in a good way. The annoying ring returned, erupting in my ears. The lights dimmed as my thoughts grew colder, darker. Full of anger and spite, they erupted in my head. The voices were raspy and sinister. "Kill. Strangle. Destroy. Pasce eam porcos." What was the last one I heard?

Mrs. Righetti scolded Mom like a child. Anger burst and spread instantly through my chest, arms, and legs. "Leave my mom alone!"

Her hand slapped my face.

I glared at her. Did a fierce growl emerge from my throat? Everyone, even Mom, stood and stepped back from me – then they all stared. What was going on?

Mom's finger, like a gun, pointed angrily at Mrs. Righetti. Even though she didn't scream or yell, Mom's short, enunciated words delivered a blunt hit to Mrs. Righetti.

"Don't you ever, ever touch my son like that again!"

Mr. Winter gently clasped Mom's arm, and Mrs. Righetti's lawyer gently clasped hers. Both sat down. I could tell Mom's anger remained. Her glaring eyes – like a tiger – projected it. Also, I could see that one vein in her forehead became prominent. Her jaw had tightened. The taut muscles in her arms and shoulders flexed. "Donna – I will pay for the medical costs – including any corrective surgery for his eye and his tooth. And Lillian suggested

10 to 20 percent above those costs for pain and suffering."

Except for Mom and Lillian, everyone else scooted away from me – at least it seemed like it. Looking at the carpet again, their voices faded, lost to the buzz that found its way back into my head. Although they talked, I never heard a word, unable to tell what they discussed. The irritating high-pitched squeal grew. I glanced over at Mrs. Righetti. The room swayed and the images blurred. Her face broke out with bruises and bloodiness. A sneer, both in my eyes and mouth, spread across my face, delivering a frightful gaze. Mrs. Righetti watched it for a split second, but terrified, she looked away.

Mom looked at me smiling. She said something – but it sounded like something said from a cave or a well. The ringing got louder – like a loud, sharp whistle. Mom's eyelids narrowed. Her face pulled in, defining wrinkles near her eyes and mouth. She kept saying something to me, but I could not hear it. Her lips seemed to say my name, followed by 'What's wrong?' The pitch was so high, I shut my eyes hoping that might blot it out. I tried covering my ears, but that did not help. The pain in my eardrums made me flinch. Maybe having my earbuds too loud hurt my hearing? Suddenly, I heard things easier: the conversation, the vents blowing warm air, and the ticking of the clock.

Everyone focused on me: the lawyers, the Righetti's and Lillian. The color faded from her cheeks, and their eyes lost a tint of color. It was weird how Mom and Lillian never said another word to me the rest of the day. They were not upset with me – just nervous. Why?

Nothing's Free

I stared at the TV but could not hear it. The high-pitched shriek in my ears irritated me to no end, vibrating heavily in my head. When it faded or disappeared, whispers emerged. What were they saying? What was the plot? Hell – what show is this, anyway? I wanted to turn up the volume on the TV, but not really paying attention I could not find the will to do it. Even worse, something kept me still, pushing into my elbows to keep me from rising or even lifting my arms. I kept seeing things in the corners of my eyes. Shadows? I kept thinking I saw Dad.

"Jeffrey?"

Mom, waving her hand in front of my face, somehow broke the spell that had wrapped around me. I cringed when reality returned, hitting me bluntly with a cold, hard slam. My head still hurt, but at least the unpleasant ringing disappeared.

She shuffled a few steps back. Over the last few days, Mom kept her distance. I picked up that she was not disappointed or angry with me – but scared. It was not just the typical over-worrying that Mom engaged in. For

94

some reason, she had withdrawn her kisses on my forehead, or her pushing my hair away from my eyes. Even Elise seemed distant. Whenever I caught her looking at me, she turned away quickly.

Needing a friend, I glanced at Freddy. He chewed on his bone. "Hey, Freddy, come here, boy." My dog looked at me, barked once, then whimpered. He walked into the other room with his tail tucked between his legs. What was with him? Come to think of it, he had not slept in my bed for the last four or five days. Even my own dog doesn't like me. Deflated, I sighed.

"Jeffrey …" I looked at Mom, "Elise and I have noticed that you … stare off somewhere for minutes on end. When you look at us, it really creeps us out. I know you're having some sort of pain. I can see it when you flinch because of something. You did get a head injury, you know. I need to know because … I can't help thinking that … all or much of this could be related to that blow you got on your head."

I never thought of that. And that damn ringing returned. It made me squirm. I flinched. Why won't this stop? It irritated me endlessly. It rang at night, during the day, while trying to do schoolwork on my laptop, and it even drowned out the music I listened to on my earbuds. Sometimes I'd be in Dad's living room chair in a trance.

No matter where I went, the place seemed darker. It felt like things rocked back and forth, like when I was on that cruise with Mom and Dad last summer.

My insides shook, even reaching the underside of my skin and forcing the hair on my arms to stand. The trance acted like this for minutes – or longer. That is, until Elise tried to ask me something. She would gently touch my arm which shattered the daze.

"There it is again," said Mom. "What is it?" She gently touched my wrist with one hand and turned off the small TV with the other one. "Jeffrey," she said, taking my hand, "my God, your hands are freezing cold and you're shaking like a leaf." She brushed my hair away. "Sweetie, please tell me."

I cried a bit. "I don't know. I hear a ringing in my ears. It sometimes hurts. I get this headache that pounds. I …" embarrassed, I wasn't sure I could say it, "I hear voices and noises. Sometimes I think something's watching me. I keep seeing things in the corners of my eyes. I'm shaking, but it's like underneath my skin. I think there's something wrong with me." The room appeared to darken. Following it was a huge terror. My stomach churned and lifted sharply like going down a roller coaster. "Mom, I'm really scared."

It was quiet for a long time. A minute? Five minutes? An hour? Strangely, the thick, heavy stillness magnified the apprehension in me.

Fear, worry, sadness, and love mixed together in Mom's face. "Jeffrey … I need to tell you something about your grandfather – the one on your dad's side. You know he died when your dad was only 16, but what you don't know is that … well … he had schizophrenia. We kept this from you and Elise, but now it seems like the time to tell you that … because … with that history of mental disease in our family, it might pass on to you."

"What's schizo … what??"

"Schizophrenia. It's a … serious mental disease."

I felt all the blood leave my face. Things slightly spun around me, and the house seemed to lean forward as shadows in the corners grew. "I'm going crazy?"

"Not crazy," she said while grasping and rubbing my hands as if trying to warm them. "A mental disease." She tried to hold back her tears. "Sometimes … mental diseases are genetically passed on. Sometimes it skips a generation. So, you, or Elise," Mom took a deep breath, "might get it." Tears escaped, dripping down the inner corners of her eyes. "I think the trauma of your father's death might be triggering it – or when you hit your head on the rock." Mom paused and hunched her shoulders. "Maybe both."

She took a sip of her wine. Then another. And another. I got worried. Should I talk to Elise about it? Should I call someone? Maybe Father Matthew? I didn't like watching Mom drink like this. It had been a very long time since I saw her drunk. When she and Dad got drunk, they would laugh and be silly. However, I knew a lot of people who drank did so to cover their emotions of anger, stress, and depression. I hoped she wasn't doing that. "Mom," I asked, quietly, "why are you drinking wine a lot more? Ever since Dad died ... I've noticed ..."

Her hand left a burning sting on my face. I think her ring may have nicked me, too. Shocked, scared, I cried. "Oh, God, sweetie, I'm sorry." She hugged me tightly. "I'm so sorry." She sobbed. "I'm so, so sorry. Please forgive me. Please."

Sis' jaw dropped, freezing like a statue. After a minute, her cheeks, eyes, and forehead relaxed.

Mom whispered. "I'll try to stop. I'm so stressed with everything going on. I'm so sorry."

"I'm sorry, too."

We both wept for a minute or two. Usually when she hugged me, bad feelings, anxiety, and fear retreated – but this time they remained stubborn. Mom backed away to face me. After brushing my bangs back, she cradled my jaw. "We're all mourning together. We need to be there for each other."

"Okay."

Mom stood and walked to the kitchen sink. Usually, I helped Elise clear the table and hand Mom the dishes. Instead, frozen, I remained at the table. Guilt, fear, and depression mixed into an undefined emotion that pulled me down into … some … darkness.

Mental illness? What would happen to me? Would I have to live in an insane asylum? Would I have to visit Psychiatrists on end for the rest of my life? Could I get a job? Would I hurt anyone – like Elise or Mom?

"And kids, the insurance money from your father's death won't arrive soon. I've had to take off from work a lot lately, so I need to get to the motel and manage it like I'm paid to do. Mr. Grayson has been very gracious to give me the days off and pay me for what he can afford. Between that, medical bills, lawyer's fees, and other things … I think we're going to have to sell the house and move in town."

Elise showed no emotion, but my head dropped – allowing my tears to hit the floor. Sometimes I thought that when we were both in Mom's womb, we made an agreement that I do all the emotions, and she would be the logical one.

I love this place. The shed was where Dad and I worked together and built motors and had fun. It was the best memories of him and now I had to give it up. I knew a lot of the financial burden had come from me in medical bills and lawyer fees. "I'm sorry, Mom. It's all my fault. I'm sorry."

"Don't say that." She enunciated every word. Wrapping her arms around me again, she hugged tightly. "It's not your fault. We will get through this together."

Was she trying to convince me, or herself?

After cleaning the kitchen, Mom poured herself more wine. "Mom?" She looked at me. My thoughts emanated from my eyes to do the talking. She nodded, then poured her wine glass empty.

About ready for bed, I looked for Freddy. Where was he? "Freddy. Come here, boy. Freddy?" I looked in the kitchen, then the living room, and the den, calling out his name. "Freddy. Where are you?" There! He was in the laundry room. "Freddy," I said, "it's time for bed. Come on."

Startled by a short growl and a sharp bark, I stepped back. Freddy backed away and whimpered – just like every night for the last week. Frustrated, I reached to pick him up, but Freddy squirmed and whined like a puppy. Something whispered. What was it saying? The lights retreated to shadows. Was someone watching me? I turned around, trying to find who or what stalked me. Just out of reach, I kept turning my head like the water draining in a sink or toilet bowl. My stomach shook, but then shrank and tightened into an icy cube.

Still trying to hold onto Freddy, I took a step forward. Terror exploded as I saw the images. First, I saw Dad. His furrowed brow, narrowed eyes, and matted beard suggested a deranged mind. Within a second, it turned into something grotesque. No. It was just my own reflection in the mirror. I dropped Freddy, and he darted away.

I took a few deep breaths. Feeling calmer, I hunched my shoulders, wondering what was wrong with Freddy. I put some food and water in his bowls, but he kept away – staring at me. I turned and left the laundry room, finally hearing the pitter-pat of his feet. It sounded like he lapped up the water furiously.

A thought or voice rushed into my mind. *"Kill him. Cook him. Feed him to Elise and Mom."* I turned. A deadly quiet stilled the air. Did that voice come from behind me – or was it inside my head? Tense, my jaw quivered. The hair on my arms and legs got cold and straightened. Trembling spread from my heart, causing it to beat uncoordinated. A tingling sensation enveloped my body, making my hands shake. Closing my eyes, I took a few deep breaths, then let them out slowly. I recited the prayer Father Matthew taught me. As my eyes opened, the uneasy feeling lost power.

Back upstairs, I looked around my room as the feeling returned. Or did Freddy sneak into the room? No. Was something out of place or missing? No – all my action figures, posters, collectibles, books were in their usual spots. My trophies for winning minibike races all gleamed in glory. However, their light diminished. Was the metal scuffed? Or did it lose its reflective quality?

Scanning the ceiling, it seemed darker, with shadows moving back and forth. I kept looking over my shoulder, turning to the right, circling myself. My eyes glanced everywhere, trying to find something … anything that might be stalking me. A frozen breath paralyzed me as I saw glowing eyes staring at me from the darkened closet. The door, ajar, opened more, letting in chilly air that circled me. The eyes swiveled to the right – but then pivoted to the left. A stinking breath pushed through my nose and mouth. I gagged and gasped, which stifled my scream. Stepping back, I fell into my chair.

A long squeak moaned like a ghost as the door opened wider. Elise! She stepped into the light. Sighing, I shook my head.

"Jesus, Elise."

What was wrong with her? She glared at me.

"Sis, please don't do that. I'm stressed as it is."

Never blinking, Elise's head tilted right, then straightened, then turned to the left.

A hand touched my shoulder. My insides jumped as my body stiffened. Turning, Elise appeared. A startled grunt heaved out my chest. Wait? What? How could she be …? The eeriness faded when I looked back at the closet. Nothing was there. I turned around, facing her again.

"Good. You should be afraid of me." Her usual tone also came with her typical emotionless eyes.

I relaxed somewhat as I shook my head. I couldn't figure out how I saw two of her. Holy shit! Two Elises in my life? That would be hell on Earth! A sigh cleared my thoughts and put out the fear.

"Are you going crazy like Mom said?"

My voice got stuck as if something invisible clutched my throat. What the fuck was going on? The tension mounted high, then diminished. "Shit! Don't sneak up on me like that. I'm stressed as it is."

"Snapping at me indicates you need electro-shock therapy," she said. "I'll push the buttons because I've always wanted to do that to you. How much voltage is the threshold?

"Knock it off, Lizzy Borden." I wished my angry voice would punch her nose.

"You two need to stop fighting," said Mom. "Now give me your phones and get to bed."

After we gave our phones to Mom, she and Elise left. I shut the bedroom and the closet doors. The uneasy feeling of someone watching me returned. Strange eyes hid somewhere, slicing through my chest with anger, hate, and fear. Closing my eyes, I dammed the tears. I inhaled deeply, held my breath for a few seconds, and let it out slowly. After several breaths, my heart relaxed. It slowed more when I said a prayer Father Matthew taught me.

I crawled into bed and pulled the covers over my shoulder. I turned to my side and shut my eyes. Sleep pulled me deep so fast that I drifted like a helium filled balloon. I heard voices, but what were they saying?

Something yanked me from my sleep, throwing me back into my mind. My eyes opened and widened as it stood over me. The size was at least six feet tall. The head possessed no mouth and had snake-like eyes with a yellowish glow. The arms were long, and shoulder blades jutted up. At the end of the arms were three fingers that resembled talons of a hawk or falcon.

My skin shriveled and contorted as its arms penetrated my chest. As it dug deeper in me, it left a chilling cold that penetrated my skin, muscles, and bones. My screams turned into muffled grunts and coughs. Frozen, terrified, I shivered as it dug through my skin. I tried to scream, but the horror wrapped around my mind and throat. A cold darkness swallowed me.

Sick Things

I woke up soaked in sweat. My perspiration drenched the sheets – even turning my pillow into a sponge. I tried to sit up, but too weak, I could only roll over. I tried to get out of bed again, but dizziness circled my brain. The windows and walls swirled, bounced, shook, and closed in. Closing my eyes, I took a few deep breaths hoping to calm everything. Even with shut eyelids, the dizziness persisted – causing me to fall on the floor.

"Mom," I whispered. I had to say it louder. "Mom! Sis!" How was I hot and cold at the same time? My dry tongue and mouth had a horrible bitter taste. I tried flexing my saliva glands, but they offered no moisture. I cringed when the familiar and horrible high-pitched ringing returned to my ears. A numbing pain swelled in my throat, forcing me to cough. More followed, refusing to stop for a minute or so. Every cough magnified the pain in my head and joints. Something felt like it wanted to escape by making my head explode. This was worse than when I got Covid. "Mom! Mom!"

The door flung open. Mom stood over me and gasped. The back of her fingers touched my forehead. "Oh, my God. You're burning up." She rushed out and quickly returned with a thermometer. She shoved it in my mouth and started drying me with a towel. "Elise," she yelled, "I need your help. Jeffrey, sit up, please."

I tried, but I even struggled to do that.

Mom took the thermometer out of my mouth. She gasped after looking at it. "Holy shit – 102." She took a deep breath then whispered, "Oh, God – what do I do? What do I do?" Mom's voice faded.

"Mom," said Elise, "what is it …" Sis gasped. "Holy Mary Mother May I!"

"Strip his bed," said Mom.

"Eww – is this sweat? Yuck!"

"Just yank them off and put them on the floor – then get some fresh linens from the closet." Mom kept patting me dry. She gasped. "My, God, Jeffrey? What's happening to your arms? They look like … something has grabbed you?"

Forcing my eyelids open, I glanced at my elbows and upper arms. Misshapen bruises, and cuts, marred my skin. Seeing them immediately made them throb. What the fuck was happening to me?

It got worse as flashes spread like lightning through my mind. For a split second, I saw a blackened room, followed by an eerie sunrise that glared through the windows. It went dark again as an orange moon appeared. Darkness returned and shadows draped over me. Another flash exploded brilliant light which made me close my eyes. Mom and Elise's voices sounded as if they talked from inside a cave. The echoes resonated louder, almost rupturing my eardrums. As the daylight returned to normal, so did their voices.

"Elise," Mom's voice now warped. No longer echoing, the tone changed, becoming low and her words stretched to a point I could barely understand. "Put the new sheets on the bed. Then get some Tylenol and water and give some to your brother."

My eyes rolled backwards. Looking up, I saw something hovering over me. It had a dark, thin image with long arms reaching down to press my head. The … thing stared at me with red, slanted, and sinister eyes. It seemed to say something – but I could not understand it. Was something crushing my skull from the outside or did something inside press out with unbelievable strength? I didn't care. I just wanted the pain to stop. "Mom," I said while almost crying, "stop the pain. Please."

The place went dark again. My arms reached out for something to grab, but they found nothing. I thudded on the floor and started twitching. Unable to stop shaking, I screamed more. "Mom, Dad, please help me. It hurts and it won't stop." Remembering Dad had died, I sobbed.

Snapping my eyes open, my whole body cringed. The thing towered over Mom! It was the same misshapen creature I saw a few seconds ago – and last night. The red eyes glared brighter, and its mouth opened, revealing two twisted fangs. It blared a violent, loud growl. "Mom! Look out. It's behind you!" My head darted back and forth, up, and down. Where was it? Panicked, I had to find it. Or did I imagine it? "Mom! Mom! I saw it. It was going to get you!"

It vanished as her head swiveled. "Sweetie, nothing's there." She whispered "sh" several times. "Jeffrey, calm down." I heard her cry. "I'm taking you to the Emergency Room. Can you stand up?"

A frigid cold wrapped around me, causing me to shiver. I retreated into a ball, hoping to find some warmth. Every few seconds, sleep tried to kidnap me, but I resisted because I did not want the nightmares to return. I could not remember them, but I did recall the horror. Mom pulled me up and wrapped her arms around me, but her hug was not enough to alleviate both the chill and despair.

Elise returned, standing next to Mom with a glass of water and some pills. Their faces lost color as their eyes sprung open. Jumping back, their screams exploded like a burst of thunder. Elise dropped the glass, shattering it into tiny beads of glass, ice, and water on the floor and my feet.

What scared them?

On the bridge between sleep and waking up, my mind scrambled. Too many images of horrific sights kept flashing through my mind, alternating between reality and dark terror. Ugly, misshapen heads, with scars and burnt skin on their faces moaned in searing heat and fire. The high-pitched noise in my ears reminded me of fingernails on a chalkboard.

It stopped. More awake, I noticed all the things attached to me. I had a needle in my left arm, connected to a tube that fed me with some liquid. Someone put another needle near my left wrist – which connected to a tube that also delivered medicine into my veins. Another thing attached to my finger, although I could take it off. A small hose wrapped around my head, over both ears and had two outlets inserted in my nostrils. Probably the most annoying thing was something inserted into my penis that connected to a bag.

Mom's face was so taut, yet somehow sweat beaded from her brow and tears fell from her eyes. "Dr. Cox – what's wrong with my son? I don't want to lose him after losing my husband. God, I miss him so much." Her voice cracked with worry as it devolved into sobs.

"Jenny," Dr. Cox gave her a one-armed hug, "please listen. I can't imagine what this is like for you, and I know you're scared." His voice was soft yet determined with confidence. "Let me tell you what we've found. It's serious, but treatable, and he's improving."

She hung on every word from the doctor. I could tell she wanted to clutch his arm, probably thinking his touch had healing powers.

"Jenny, it looks like Jeffrey is stabilizing. We put him on an IV to help with the dehydration, and another to trigger urination and it's working," he added, looking at that bag. "His creatine levels were high, and so far, we have not found any indication of infection either with respiratory or bloodborne pathogens."

Mom looked more confused. What worried me more was that Dr. Cox appeared to be the most puzzled. "The perplexing part is that it seems like his body is going through some sort of rejection – like if Jeffrey got an organ transplant."

"What's that mean?" I mumbled.

Dr. Cox moved closer and took my pulse, then looked at all the machines. "When people get organ transplants, the body will try to reject it because it wasn't originally their own organ. But you haven't had any transplants – so I doubt that's it. I just can't figure out what kind of sickness you have."

"Dr. Cox," I hesitated, "I'm not going to die, am I?"

"Let me tell you the good news: your urine production is up, your fever has gone down, and your O2 levels are looking much better," he said while pushing my fingernails. He then clasped my forearm which pushed back the subtle anxiety bubbling under my skin. "Jeffrey – you better not die on me because that'd make me look bad and I hate looking bad," he said while tapping my head with a clipboard. The smile across his face passed me a slight grin. "So, we're going to figure this one out so I can be praised and exalted by your family and my peers – because I only care about looking good in front of others." My grin changed to a chuckle. "Is there anything else you wish to tell me right now – other than how awesome a doctor I am."

Losing my smile, I tried to use my tongue like a sponge to squeeze out some saliva. "My mouth feels mega dry."

"Give the IV time to push back dehydration. And I'll see to it you get some more ice water."

"Hey, dude." I smiled as Gunner came over and grabbed my hand.

"Oh, God," I whispered. "I'm so glad to see you."

"Mom brought me over. I heard what happened and was really worried."

"He insisted," said Aunt Beth.

"What is it, dude?"

"I don't know." I coughed. "The doctors don't know, either." After a few more coughs, I could speak again. "It's pissing me off." My anger faded, making my voice trail. "And …" my voice changed to a whisper, "well … I'm really scared."

He hugged my upper torso. "You gotta get better. We gotta hit the minibike races soon. The season's just around the corner."

"I know." I grunted, then coughed again. "Thanks, dude."

Gunner gasped, abruptly stopped hugging me, and backed away.

"Gunner," said Elise. "I'm glad you're at the hospital. Remember that surgery we discussed on Halloween? I can perform it in operating room four in about thirty minutes." It was amazing how she stayed in character for that joke.

"Elise!" Mom glared at her.

"Mom, I must practice my castration techniques. I'll just remove one testicle. I promise." She hesitated. "Besides, he has two."

Mom shook her head after rolling her eyes at Elise. My sister stood in front of me. "So, what's it like after crossing over into death and then coming back? Did you see the light? Or did it go dark and spit you back?"

I let loose a weak smile. I shook my head and released a few coughs. "Actually, death told me 'wrong kid – we wanted the other one.'"

"You had me worried," she said. "Think about it: if you died – my chore list would double." Elise's smile, as usual, barely broke, only on one side. She hugged my shoulders and kissed me on the head. "I'm glad you're better."

"Young Jeffrey ..." Sister Regina's smile spread across her mouth, pressed into her cheeks, and made her eyes widen. Even her face brightened as she spoke. "I heard my favorite and most handsome young parishioner was horribly sick."

I started to smile, but the ringing exploded in my ears as I looked in her eyes. My eyes clamped hard as if something pressed against them from inside my head. Inhuman screams, growling, and echoes overwhelmed the ringing. I shuddered as a hot, stinking breath covered me. Freezing, I clutched my arms. Someone, or rather something put their arms around me. The embrace sickened me as a putrid smell triggered my gag reflex. Its arms had dry pieces of skin flaking onto me and my hospital gown. Long and disfigured fingers clamped around my throat and squeezed. Struggling for breath, I coughed, but nothing could escape my lungs. Panicked, I coughed more, shuffled my legs. Who was screaming? Mom? Aunt Beth?

Inside my mind, it showed up again. The tall form let loose its hollow stare that actually punched me. Its body dripped some mucous-like substance so gross and dirty that its smell made me gag. The long, deformed arms twisted in bizarre ways and slapped me. My eyes burst open as the vice on my neck now clamped on my testicles. It spoke to me, but I heard its words explode from my mouth. "Get away from me! Feed them to the pigs!" What? What did I say? I mean – I heard it in my mind, but that did not match the words out of my mouth.

The room, now dark, still showed everyone's outline. Mom, Aunt Beth, Gunner, and Elise had backed against the wall with Sister Regina. The nun had her crucifix and beads in one hand – while stretching her other arm to protect the rest. A vicious growl erupted out of my mouth. Mom and Aunt Beth both draped their arms tightly around Elise and Gunner's shoulders and stomach. The color in all their eyes faded as their skin whitened as the lights flickered on and off.

Something inside swallowed me, drowning my soul and in a deep, dark pool. Suffocating, I kicked and swam as hard as I could to break the surface and inhale some air. Reaching the top, my mouth opened and tried to take in some fresh air – but I choked on some water. Then, something underneath pushed me violently into some sort of … blackness.

Shocked, I hovered over my body. It looked up at Mom, Aunt Beth, and Sister Regina and seemed to bellow a low, loud noise at them. It sounded muffled – but what was going on? How could it do that if I … wasn't in my body? Was this real? A nightmare? In a panic, I tried to return to my physical being by flailing my arms and legs – but I barely moved. Desperate, I …

tried ... swimming through the air – but could not get any closer. More panicked, terrified, I almost cried as I tried harder to return to my body. Although I was out in the open, I felt trapped, alone, and desperate. I tried harder to return. What's happening? Suddenly, something pulled me back in, as if falling down a steep slide.

Confused, my thoughts scrambled as I felt my body return – or did I return to it? My breaths raged, almost hurting my chest. Fingers, hands, arms, toes, legs, knees all shook, and sweat seeped heavily through my skin.

Sister Regina relaxed her stance and moved closer to me. Lifting my chin, she glanced lightly. Her hand made the holy cross motion, and she prayed in Latin, but I understood it. "Father God, protect this child of yours with the patronage of the angels."

Unable to respond, all I could do was stare straight ahead. I wanted to ask for help, but I lay there unable to move. Why can't I move? I tried to move a finger or a toe, but nothing responded. Unable to even blink, I panicked again, trying to move, speak even harder – but I could only breathe. *Why can't I move?* The thought screamed in my mind.

I heard a subtle, coarse voice respond.

"Because I'm in control."

Glancing around, I tried to find someone – anyone – who might have said that. Nothing. I resided alone in a black empty void that had a still, eerie silence.

"My place now."

"Who are you?" I thought.

"I am made of you."

"You're me?"

"No, I'm made of you. Soon, you will no longer be. Now, this is my place."

Did it disappear? The loneliness and emptiness had me so quiet, I could hear my heartbeat. Where'd he … it go? *"Are you still there? Who are you? Come back. I need answers. You're scaring me."* No response. Strangely, while the icy presence vanished, the fear of being alone seemed just as terrifying. I also wanted some answers and the thing had them.

Taking in a heavy breath, I saw a light that swung away.

"Jeffrey?"

Looking at Dr. Cox. "Yes, sir?" Tears streamed. "What happened?"

His blue eyes looked concerned – especially when he tilted his head and crossed his arms. "I was hoping you'd be able to tell me. You've been unresponsive for almost four-and-a-half hours."

Thinking about it, not only did a cold uncertainty fall through, but also a blunt embarrassment. Did I really have a conversation with another personality? A few more tears fell as I wondered what to say.

"Jeffrey? What's going on, son?"

I hesitated. "Where's mom?"

He paused. "Your aunt took your mother home. She was on the verge of a nervous breakdown, so I prescribed a sedative for her." Dr. Cox sighed. "Can you tell me if you remember anything from your episode?"

Should I tell him I was kicked out of my body? Or of the conversation I had with the … thing inside me? Afraid, I stared at my feet. "No," I whispered. "I don't remember anything." My voice trailed as my thoughts gathered. "Dr. Cox … I'm really scared."

"I understand. I'm sorry you're going through this." His voice was quiet. "I'm sorry I haven't been much help. I wish I could do more."

"I feel so alone. I really miss Dad."

Dr. Cox touched my shoulder. "I know you do."

I grabbed his arm, hoping to pull him closer. Dr Cox hugged me tightly. "Let it all out, son," he said quietly.

Identity Crisis

Sitting in my own bed, I quivered. No matter how much I prayed or crossed myself, the tension pressed against me. My fingers, toes, and my skin trembled – even affecting the hairs on my skin. The terror of the unfamiliar creature paralyzing me lingered in my mind.

My vision blurred like when summer heat lifted off the hot pavement. My lungs locked a breath as the creature appeared. I assumed it was the thing that talked to me in the pit of my mind. Suddenly, the apparition changed to a darkened silhouette that somehow emanated colors. The image pressed tighter together as distinguishing features such as skin color, hair, and clothes took shape. The beard was the first giveaway. "Dad?"

"Yes, son?"

His voice distorted, along with his image. Both disintegrated into fine particles of sight and sound – and had disappeared and I fell back into my pillow. Shaking my head, I inhaled, held my breath, and slowly let it out. The dizziness and confusion weakened enough so I could think and stave off my crying.

Elise walked into the room with a glass of ice water. "Here," she said quietly. She backpedaled quickly after I took it with both hands to keep it stable. I gulped the water heavily, as if yanking it into the deepest part of me. The icy water felt wonderful as it refreshed my tongue, mouth, and poured through my esophagus into my stomach. The water kept falling deep, not quite finding – or filling the dark emptiness inside. Why won't the water refresh me fully, and fill me with something good? Why was I so thirsty?

Elise started to leave.

"Sis, wait." I cried. "Don't leave me. I don't know what's happening to me and I'm really scared. Am I going crazy – or am I just sick?" I'm not too sure if I expected an answer from her – but I needed to let my fear be known to someone. "Why is this happening to me?" I hope she understood me as my voice cracked and devolved into sobs.

Looking up, I saw it appear. It was behind Elise's shoulder! The empty eyes, strips of flesh across the hideous mouth, the red, blistering skin, and mucous falling from the slits that worked as a nose. Its long arms lifted, displaying the misshapen talons. They reached for her neck. "Don't hurt my sister! Leave her alone!"

Elise stepped back as her eyes widened with terror. Her skin whitened, almost resembling the appearance of a corpse. Her voice exploded. "Jeffrey – no!" She rushed backwards, slamming into my minibike trophies and action figures that all fell to the floor. "Please don't hurt me!" Her breaths were short, quick, nervous bursts. I'd never seen so much emotion from her.

"What is going on with you two?" Mom's unique voice somehow mixed bass and soprano. It gave it a punch that frightened both of us when angry.

"Mom – please! He's scaring me. I don't want to be around Jeffrey. He always looks like he wants to kill me or something."

The words triggered more crying. "I don't want to hurt you. I love you," I hope they understood me. "I'm so scared. The buzzing won't stop in my head – I'm hearing voices and seeing horrible things. I feel like something's always watching me. I feel so alone and confused. Please don't hate me."

Stunned silent, both Mom and Elise hesitated – likely to think about what to say next. Sis took another step back, then wiped the tears off her cheeks. Was she embarrassed, or scared? She inhaled deeply, then blurted it out. "Sometimes," she stammered, "I think … you're … someone or … something else. It scares me." Her voice weakened. Elise rushed forward and wrapped her arms around me. "I'm sorry," she whispered. This time, I heard heartfelt emotion. "I'm so sorry. I wish I knew what to do."

Mom sat on the bed, rubbing my back, and pushing my hair away from my eyes. Mom's face, riddled with worry, fear, and pain looked at me and wept. "Sweetie …" she stuttered a couple of breaths. "We're going to help you. I promise. Okay? I'm not going to let anything bad happen to you." It was her turn to embrace me. Although warm, it seemed pale to the cold inside my stomach and chest. It felt like ice – as if I were freezing from the inside-out. I wanted to tell her about the … whatever it was … kicking me out of my body, and the conversation I had with it. Scared, I said nothing.

"I'm not going to let anything bad happen to you."

I clenched my eyes so tight, it hurt. I wanted to believe Mom, but it sounded too much like she tried to convince herself.

Nobody Likes Me

Watching Aunt Beth drive the car, I smiled. If Mom wasn't around, I could always count on my aunt. She was like my second mom. She had reddish hair that she kept short. Although she was a bit heavier, her body was not obese – or even fat. She was always reliable and available to everyone – especially Mom. Sometimes I think she helped to make-up for Uncle Walt being a jerk to Dad, Mom, and me. I noticed a lot of men referred to their wives as their better half, but I think Aunt Beth was Uncle Walt's better two-thirds – or maybe his better nine-tenth.

Aunt Beth offered to take me to the Psychiatrist today to help Mom who needed to manage the motel the last few days to make up for lost time. Gunner was in the back with me. He acted very weird today, glancing at me in short bursts, then looking at his phone. His eyes and face indicated he was afraid, and his fingers trembled. He inhaled deeply, then spoke his words fast and sharp. "You okay, dude?" He appeared reluctant, but moved closer, tapping me on the shoulder. "You okay, Jeffrey?"

My head turned sharply, casting an angry glare that pushed him back to the other side of the back seat. Spooked, Gunner retreated, still glancing at me but quickly looking away.

My eyes locked on the windshield. The light outside faded – as if heavy clouds suddenly shielded the sun. It reminded me of that total eclipse that happened a few years ago.

Something seized my identity, or perhaps cast it aside. Feeling a cold, sinister presence inside, my vision tunneled. The noise of the car, Aunt Beth and Elise's conversation had muffled, sounding like it drowned in the water. The whispering voices became louder, also reverberating and distorting. The presence felt angry, spiteful, and hateful. It was so reprehensible, I fought hard, hoping to push it out of me. Stubborn, the personality glared at Gunner. Was I sneering at him?

"Shit, boys! Did one of you roll down a window?"

"No, Mom," said Gunner. He retreated, glanced at me, then back at his phone. "I thought one of you did. Can you turn up the heat a bit?"

My whole body panged as something took control of me. The sensation reminded me of when the thing paralyzed my soul and kicked me out of my body. My mind scrambled, as if trying to resist the ugly, cold power. *"Please not again. Please not again. Please not again."* The thought echoed so many times I lost count.

It happened again. My personality, self, and identity felt pushed aside. No longer in charge, I could only be a spectator. Confused, scared, my … spirit or soul panicked and tried to find power once again. Finding none, my soul desperately jumped and flailed to regain dominance. At the same time, a bitter, freezing cold emanated within my chest. It weighed my being down, pushing me away from my mind.

The sun darkened, but no clouds blocked it. The darkness cast a cold emptiness within me. It spread to my joints, limbs, and even my fingers and toes. Reality appeared like a tunnel, growing massively in length and swirling. My insides lifted. Was I going to drown in this darkness? Something weighed me down, making it hard to remain in the light. Anxiety and panic paralyzed my thinking. How did I get here? I cried out, but my voice echoed back – hurting my ears.

Like a slingshot – something launched me forward. I found light again. Something inside me, angry, spiteful, and malicious blurted through my mouth. "I heard you like to have abortions."

What? That wasn't my voice. It was harsh, deep, and raspy.

"Mommy?" The new voice coming from me sounded like a child – perhaps a little girl. "Why did you kill me?"

Aunt Beth, terrified and panicked, turned sharply, taking the car off the road and into the field. Gunner and I bounced up and down and side-to-side. Aunt Beth slammed on the brakes, lurching us forward, slamming us into the backseat and then on each other.

I heard Aunt Beth downstairs whispering angrily to Mom. Wait! How could I do that? Was I floating out of my body again?

"Jenny – how could you tell him about that?" She cried as her hands shook while cradling a glass of wine.

"I never told him anything about it. I promise you."

"Well, how the hell did he find out? It was painful enough to decide and I confided in you. I never even told my parents that … or even Walt."

"Beth," said Mom, "I swear that I never told Jeffrey – or anyone about that abortion."

Their voices sounded strange, as if they rode some waves through a choppy sea. They cried a little, put their glasses down, and hugged each other. I felt really bad. Why would I say anything like that?

"Jenny," Aunt Beth pulled away from the hug. "I hate to tell you this – but … Jeffrey … scared the shit out of me and Gunner." She shook her head. "It was a sense of … fear or dread. And for a split second, I looked in the rear-view mirror and … I saw," she closed her eyes and whispered, "something I can't describe. It was so … disgusting. Hideous. Evil. I could have sworn I heard a growl. And it chilled me to the bone. There's something not right about him. Jeffrey glares at me, at Gunner. His eyes … do they seem darker to you? Well, his face is so taut, and fierce like he's planning to … hurt us."

Was I floating above Mom and Aunt Beth? Confused, I wondered where my body was. Am I even in it? Was I pushed out again? How could I get back in? Abruptly, something yanked me back into my bedroom and awakened from a stupor when I saw a hand pass before my eyes.

"Dude," said Gunner, "are you okay? Elise told me you've been drinking water like crazy. Here's some for … you." His voice trailed as he kept his distance, while handing me the large glass. He froze and his skin whitened. Did I sneer at him? His arms and hands tensed, then he stepped back, dropped the water, and fell.

It felt weird as I grew and stretched. A hard chill exploded in my stomach and lifted, dragging me higher by my rib cage. It hurt. I struggled to exhale. Within a few seconds, I towered over my cousin…was I yelling at him? Something from me slapped him in the face, knocking him back into the wall – leaving a small hole in it. He coughed. Why would I hit him? I love Gunner.

"Mom!!!" His scream, long, loud, and explosive, did not startle me. I relished it and felt immense pride. It gave me joy, making me feel powerful. Why?

Scrambling to his feet, Gunner rushed towards the door. Something within me forced me to swing my arm. Following it, a strong gust carried books, collectibles, and other objects across the room, slamming into walls and Gunner. The door slammed before he could reach it. Crying, Gunner yanked at the door and screamed. "Mom! Mom! Aunt Jenny! Help!"

The frigid cold surged in my head, causing something like an ice-cream headache. My eyes slanted and receded further back. Gritting my teeth, I laughed through them. I felt the urge to rip him apart. No! He's my best friend. *"Stop it! Stop it! Stop it!"* I repeated the thought over and over. The foreign thing inside me tried to break free and deliver another punch to Gunner. *"I said stop it!"*

The presence vanished. I stood in front of my cousin, huffing. Crying, shaking, Gunner's breath expelled erratically, out of sync, and fast. "Oh, Gunner … I'm sorry," I said crying, "I'm really sorry. Please forgive me. I didn't mean it."

The door swung open, startling me. Aunt Beth rushed in, dropped to her knees, and hugged him. Gunner grunted. "Mom, please!" he said. "My shoulder. You're hurting me." She stopped hugging and apologized. She noticed the purplish bruise and gash on his face, which dripped blood. Her angry eyes glared at me so hard, it felt like a punch in the gut that almost toppled me to the floor.

"You keep away from my son!"

Shocked, I never heard Aunt Beth yell at me like that. Her words hit me like a blunt rock. I retreated from her rage.

"Do you hear me!"

Crying, I nodded.

"Mom, Mom," interrupted Gunner, "we gotta get out of here – now!"

Aunt Beth quickly got him out while yelling back at Mom. "Keep your kid away from my son! And for fuck's sake, get that boy help – FAST." Storming away, she slammed the door so hard, a few posters and photos blew off the walls.

Mom's slap stung hard. "What the fuck do you think you're doing? Attacking your cousin like that? What's gotten into you?" I never heard her so angry. The forehead vein bulged. Fury filled her eyes, but the anger faded and changed. They grew as terror swelled within them and overflowed. Her head lifted to look at me.

The cold returned, stretching my ribcage, making it difficult to breathe. Did I grow again? Was I out of my body?

Mom's hands covered her mouth. Somewhere between anger and shock, could only gaze at me. Elise walked into the room. She dropped the linens and let loose an ear-splitting scream.

Flatline

Mom hovered over me, touched my forehead, and brushed my hair back. Her face looked so gaunt. Her brown eyes squinted, trying to hold back the flood behind her eyes as her lips curled. "Sweetie – hang on. They're going to see you now." Her voice bounced off invisible cavern walls so much, it was hard to decipher what she said.

In the hospital again, I had electrodes and wires on my forehead to measure my brain waves. Now, the doctors wanted to take an image of my head. A medical person guided me to a cold, hard table that started to retract into the MRI machine. Only wearing a stupid hospital gown added to humiliation and misery.

That damn wailing in my ears loudened, pounding my head and ears from the inside. Why can't it stop for just one fucking minute? Why won't that headache go away? No medication could rid me of this miserable pain – even those powerful ones that made me sleepy and gave me nightmares.

I felt so alone. Every time I tried to pray, the awful pain, terrible noises, and sinister whispers intensified. I grunted. Even though a nurse put some shields over my eyes, the horrid images still flashed through my mind. They overwhelmed me, burning my mind with terror.

"Okay, Jeffrey," said a voice from the intercom, "we're going to start the machine and it's going to take pictures of your head. You're going to feel some magnetic waves. Your skin, and your muscles and bones might feel like they're vibrating, but they won't harm you – although it will feel a little uncomfortable. You'll probably find the loud noise much more annoying. It should take about 20 minutes or so. I'll be giving you instructions. Are you ready?"

I stammered out my reply: "Yes, sir."

My body didn't seize, but every muscle jerked – as if being shocked. While that horrid chorus in my head retreated, the vibrations kicked in. I felt it in my bones – particularly my joints. The table was so uncomfortable. Why don't they have at least some cushions or a blanket to lie on? I don't know if it was the noise or the magnetic waves, but my ears rang loud. I felt trapped. Everything seemed to close in drastically. How long was this going to take? "Please hurry," I muttered. "I hate this. It really hurts my head." Moans and grunts leapt out of my mouth incessantly. I doubt they could hear me over all this noise the machine made, along with the magnetic waves. The circular tube seemed like a trap, and I was unable to escape. The pressure inside my head exploded as the high-pitched beeps sounded. It felt like someone was yelling from within my head, pushing out with superhuman strength.

I'm not too sure how long it lasted – but seemed like forever. As the electrical and magnetic waves ceased, I felt relief. Exhausted, I kept huffing while the small table slowly rolled me out of the tube. Mom and the technician came in to help me sit up on the edge of the table.

The pain surged through my head, like a tidal wave smashing into a shoreline. I flinched, cringed, and screamed. Mom appeared in a tunnel. She screamed, although I barely heard her as both her voice and image faded. My eyelids reacted like heavy weights as all the strength left my body and everything turned black.

My eyes opened to a blurry, bright vision that turned into a tunnel. Whisked away, I fell into some sort of pit. Spasms of pain hit me in my chest over and over. It hurt so much that I screamed – but no echoes escaped in this long cavern. Every time it hit, I saw images: Mom, Dad, Elise, Gunner, Aunt Beth, Father Matthew. Strong memories kept flashing in my mind: my 13th birthday at

Hooters in Pittsburgh, seeing "Night of the Living Dead" with my dad in the old classic theater, minibike racing, Gunner and I playing, being with Grandma and Grandpa at Lake Pittsburgh, meeting Kane Hodder and Nick Castle at Comic Con, the Alice Cooper concerts with Mom and Dad. The images vanished as the noise of the death chorus wailed, getting closer.

Something crushed my chest over and over – sending waves of pain through my torso. A stinging, fiery pain convulsed in me and spread brief flashes of light. It happened a second time, making every part of my body spasm. The pains in my chest returned, again pushing memories out with every thump. I fell back into the long, cavernous tunnel. Another burning pain exploded as a light spread and faded like a flash of lightning. My eyes sprung open.

A whole bunch of medical people surrounded me. Confused, scared, my heart pumped so fast it felt like a stampede of horses. A wincing pain radiated from my torso, making every breath a march of pain spreading throughout my chest and sides. Something burned on my chest and stomach. Hands reached down to keep me on the cold, hard table. An oxygen mask was placed over my mouth. What? Why were electrodes on my chest? A few coughs triggered some pain in my ribcage.

"He's back," said one person.

"Thank God."

"Keep an eye on his breathing."

"Full normal sinus rhythm."

"Miss – we got him."

Mom stood over me and hugged me tight. The marching pain returned. Cringing, I screamed. "Mom, stop! You're hurting me."

She let go, let me fall to the table, then hovered over me, apologizing. "I'm sorry. I'm sorry. I'm so sorry, baby." She sobbed and dropped her head onto my chest. "Please don't leave me. Please don't leave me."

Don't leave? What happened?

Why Trust You?

I cringed with every breath. The CPR broke two of my ribs. The pain had lessened – thanks to the pain medication. However, it also made me sleepy. No noises or voices in my head or in my hospital room existed – except for the monitors hooked up to electrodes on my chest and finger. I felt so alone. The quiet spread to my body. Feeling numb of all emotion, and even the pain, I didn't even shake. Would it happen again? When? For two minutes and twelve seconds – I was dead. I did not breathe, and my heart stopped, which stilled the blood in my veins.

The doctors didn't know what was wrong, finding no explanation for the death. I surely did not know what was happening. For the … hundredth time, I tried to piece everything together, hoping to solve the bizarre puzzle. None of the pieces fit.

Dark bangs partially blocked my vision. Tears welled up in my eyes, although all emotions remained at bay. With nobody else here, I dropped my head even more, desperate for any kind of help. Father Matthew always told me to say what was on my mind. "God … I don't know if you can hear me – but I'm really scared. I'm not ready to die. I want to be with Mom, Elise, Gunner, Sister Regina, and Aunt Beth. I want to do a bunch of stuff here on Earth." My voice got angry. "Why are you doing this to me? It's not fair! First, you let Dad die – and now you're going to let me die? Or go crazy? I always hear you have a plan for my life, but right now it seems like a real shitty one to me!" After my outburst, I paused for a moment. "I don't know what you want me to do. Can't you please tell me?"

"He wants you to have faith."

My head turned towards Father Matthew's voice. Although he has a bass voice, it was gentle, smooth, and soothing. It appeared genuine and real. I could listen to him teach the Bible or give a sermon anytime. It was a voice perfect for audio versions of books. The calmness often dropped fear in its tracks. On occasion, I found his voice so relaxing, I nodded off to sleep. Not that he was boring, but rather comforting. It was the best thing about Father Matthew.

Using his cane, he guided himself to a chair next to me. "I'm sorry I haven't been here sooner, Jeffrey. So many parishioners need prayer, visits, and comfort just like you. You've always been one of my favorites in the church. You have such a good heart, an open mind, a caring soul, and you're so eager to learn."

I wept a little. "I'm afraid I'm going to die." Letting loose a heavy sigh, I looked away from his eyes. I didn't feel ashamed or anything like that – but it was hard to face him when I lacked faith. Maybe that's what a priest or pastor is for. "And I think I'm going crazy. Mom told me about my grandfather on Dad's side. He had some mental illness … and I'm afraid I'm getting it, too."

"Well," he said while feeling for the chair and sitting, "I'd be scared, too, so I can understand your fear."

"I died. I was dead for over two minutes, and they brought me back. Why? So, I can go mega crazy?" I stopped, realizing my voice yelled at the one person I never wanted to yell at. I wiped the tears off my cheeks and used the tissues to wipe the snot dripping from my nose. Although it hurt, I took a deep breath, held it for a few seconds, then slowly let it out. Doing it again, I felt some peace – at least within my own body. Harmony between my lungs and heart soothed my anxiety.

"Jeffrey – it's easy to believe and have faith when things are going well. It is perfectly natural to feel that way. The hard part is having faith when things are going wrong, when we suffer, and when we go through pain."

I heard him, but I did not like the answer. "It's too much. Dad dying. And now me going nuts." I clamped my eyes shut, trying to keep from crying.

Father Matthew stood, reaching for me. I took his hand so he could find me. "Father, I could really use some prayer. I'll take all I can get."

He placed his hand on my head, his other on my shoulder. The warm touch added to the peace. His voice soothed me.

The high-pitched sound exploded as the images of hideous creatures with scabs, scars, blood, puss, and sunken eyes returned. The room spun violently – or was it me? A cold terror filled every part of me, forcing my body to shudder. A new image exploded in my head: the elongated head, the sunken eyes, the scars on the face. The vertical strands of flesh ripped as it yelled with a deep, ominous voice – or was I saying this? "Let me go, you bastard! Get out!"

The words in my mind did not match the gibberish that came out of my mouth. And the voice was evil.

Father Matthew retreated fast – slamming into the wall and falling to one side. Clutching his heart, he tried to calm it down. His mouth shot open, and his useless eyes widened in shock. Even though he could not see, terror washed over his whitened face, and he shivered.

The lights, both from the lamps and the sun, dimmed. I shook. Not just my fingers, but my skin, my hairs … and even my spirit. The anxiety circled me, like some sort of evil creature.

"Jeffrey?"

Father Matthew's voice distorted. It did not just echo, but it also morphed into a deep dissonance. Confusing, it sounded like an old scratchy record. My vision faded to a haze and turned on itself, swinging to the left. The hard motion to the right made my stomach feel queasy. Disgusting, smelly vomit erupted from my mouth. The stench was awful, and the taste was worse. It spilled on my blanket. Then, something cold revealed itself in my mind. Pushing me back, taking over, this … thing wrapped its powerful, deformed fingers around my neck and squeezed my throat. I struggled for breath. Then, my hands … or rather long, thin arms extended. The flesh flaked. A horrendous, sulfurous odor made me gag … and almost vomit again. A low, guttural growl pushed through my neck. "Get away from the dirty worm. Or I will kill this vessel and cast his soul into hell."

What? What the hell was I saying? That's not my voice! It was deep, harsh, and raspy. And what I said in my mind came out of my mouth differently, as I spoke a foreign language. I think it was Latin – but I didn't know it that well.

Father Matthew, no longer afraid, stood upright. He took a deep breath and moved closer – cautiously. His dilated eyes somehow filled with terror and shock. His mouth dropped open, spilling a breath outlined in mist. "Jeffrey, what did you say?"

I … or rather the thing inside me … subtly growled – like a dog getting ready to sic its prey. I sneered and chortled softly at Father Matthew. My body grew taller, towering over him.

Father Matthew's jaw dropped. "Oh, my God."

Welcome to my Nightmare

What? How'd I get back to my room? Strangely, the books were gone. Some of my action figures were missing. I checked the lightbulbs as the room was dim. Even the light from outside lacked brightness although I didn't see any clouds. It reminded me of those found footage horror films Dad hated. The whole place had a dark graininess to it.

Immediately, a bitter cold forced my whole body to cringe. After hugging myself and rubbing my arms, I breathed into my hands to warm them. Suddenly realizing I stood naked in the middle of the room, I quickly checked my dresser drawers, looking for something to wear. However, nothing was there. I grabbed the blankets off my bed and wrapped them around me.

I shook – not so much from the cold but rather the ominous dread that intensified and surrounded me. It slithered deep within me, crippling any hope or faith that remained. More light faded, matching the despair inside my heart and mind. Tiny sounds, like a crinkling of aluminum foil, wisped around me. The windows disappeared as the door of my room vanished. I scurried to the opposite corner as something appeared. My eyes squinted, trying to make out the dark shadow in the corner across from me.

Shadows, moving slowly and menacingly, circled me as if preparing to attack. Something like gnats flew around my head, annoying my nose, ears, and skin. They became malevolent and sinister, leaving behind stings, and a high-pitched buzzing sound in my ears. Pain stirred in my torso, my arms, legs, and head where they left stinging bites. My gasps raced – as if competing with my heartbeat.

The lights came on, startling me. Staring at the ceiling, unable to move, something descended on me fast and hard – forging control in every part of my body. Feeling its fear and anger, my insides chilled, but then instantly changed to a dry, oppressive heat. The thing inside pushed me up and flipped me, pounding my feet on the … ceiling?

I looked for the scream below and saw Elise run for the door. It felt as if a blast of wind exploded out of my mouth, slamming the door in front of my sister. Her eyes doubled in size, and all color drained from her skin. While she pounded on the door, her shrieking voice sounded as if it was trying to escape a deep, cavernous well. "Mom! Mom! Help!" She yanked the doorknob.

Wondering what was wrong, I realized a sinister grin sprawled across my face and my eyes glared at her. Fangs jutted from my upper jaw as I let loose a low growl that horrified me just as much as her. Crying, she pulled the door slightly ajar, but another howl blew the door closed. A surging hatred within erupted, forcing my arms to flex and my hands (and claws?) tighten.

I tried to fight it but could only watch as the vile hatred vibrated inside my chest. Only able to watch, the room darkened while books and minibike trophies flew across the room – resembling a whirlwind. Some things hit Elise in her face, nose, and eyes. Her cheek bruised, her facial skin reddened, and some blood leaked from lacerations. "Jeffrey, please! Please!"

I didn't want to hurt her! Why couldn't I stop? I tried to talk to her, but an icy, sinister presence froze my tongue, boxed my mind in a metal case, and pulled my eyes wide open. It howled, and even laughed, although it was more like an evil snicker. Relishing the fear it created, it spun around to celebrate, passing fear to me. The terror spread like a fire, feeding itself and intensifying.

I pushed off the ceiling, flipped, and landed on the floor. Mom opened the door, gasped, and shrieked. Her widened eyes looked painful. Clutching her chest, she backed up fast, but her scream stifled under the shock. Instinctively, she grabbed Elise and pulled her back. "Jeffrey!" she yelled, "what the hell?" Her voice twisted, echoed, and distorted into nothingness.

A deep, gravelly voice resonated from me. "It's just us. LEAVE!" The voice, so loud, exploded and carried a violent, hurricane-like gust that shoved Mom and Elise out the door.

The hoarse, sinister laugh hollowed out my insides. Cold pricks stabbed my skin and sank deep into my muscles and bone. My heart fluttered as the vile anger remained, circling, swirling, and capturing me. I wanted to remove myself from the unwanted guest, but it had my body. How could I get it out?

What was this thing? Another personality? A ghost? My twisted subconscious? It frightened me like nothing else. Chills ran through my skin, down my spine, and to the tips of my fingers and toes. Feeling trapped, alone, I freaked out, desperately wanting to get out. Get out of where? My room? My body? So confused by all the images and sensations, dizziness set in. However, closing my eyes did not help to dispel the feeling.

The horror movies Dad and I watched were not real, only imagined by screenwriters, special effects gurus, directors, and actors. They made me tense, frightened me as I thought of frightening possibilities, and startled me. However, this thing released a continuous onslaught of horrid despair and terror. Cowering, I wanted to get away – but there was nowhere to go. Trapped in my head were the voices of tormented souls, an unholy song, and the goddamn ringing! Why wouldn't that ringing in my head stop? It peaked, disturbing not just my sleep, but also my sanity. When would this stop? Would it stop? I tried to pray to God, but something invisible and strong crushed my throat. I couldn't speak or think. Although I cried, I found no tears.

The room went dark. I was in the blanket cowering in the corner again. The shadowy figure had grown. It stood ten, maybe twelve feet tall. It looked at me. The devilish, yellow eyes cut right through me. In the terror, I lost all hope and faith. Would it kill me? Take over? Would I survive as a person and be a slave to this thing? My own scream echoed in my head, desperately wanting out.

My room was light again. Everything reversed as doors and windows appeared on opposite walls. Bookcases shifted to the other side and even the colors on my bed and posters reversed, using the opposite ends of the spectrum. It was unusually bright, almost hurting my eyes.

The lights dimmed, allowing me to see … Gunner! So happy to see him, I smiled and cried. Moving forward to hug him, he panicked and backed away. "Go away!" His voice distorted, compressed, and stretched into an indiscernible deep low-pitched scream.

It was Uncle Walt. He said something angrily, but I couldn't make it out. It sounded like he was talking backwards … and that his words passed through something like water. His image also folded and blurred, like when you see heat rise off the pavement in the summer.

I felt taller. I had not grown, but something lifted me from within my chest, stretching my ribs again. Towering over Uncle Walt, I felt a surge of hate. Suddenly, a red, fuzzy, melancholy haze spread across my vision – adding to the spite within me. I lurched at him, spun, and planted my feet on the … ceiling? How do I keep doing this? Grabbing his arm, I pulled hard and heard something crack. His low, discordant scream sounded as if he yelled under the water.

Everything went dark and silent. Eyes wide open, I still could not see anything, not even the hand I waved in front of my face. Nothing. No noises existed. I carefully moved to one side, extending my arms to find a wall, a post, a bed, or anything to guide me downstairs to Mom and Elise.

My fingers touched a wall, then one of my knees hit it. As my other hand touched the wall, my fingers acted as sensors, guiding me in the dark. Shock and terror seized me, freezing my mind and soul and knotting my heart and stomach. Pounding on the walls again, I realized my ears heard nothing. I yelled as loud as I could: "Mom! Mom! Elise!" Unable to hear my own voice, terror spread, causing me to shake and cry. As the darkness and silence surrounded me, I winced, afraid to move. Wait. Just because I couldn't hear, doesn't mean I didn't make any sounds. I yelled as hard as I could for Mom or Elise. I even called for Father Matthew or Gunner – hoping they might be there to help.

Still, I reached out, hoping to find something else to guide me … or try to defend myself. My breaths came in short bursts as I feared that thing watched me. Feeling sinister eyes burn on my skin, I stayed put. Smelling its horrid breath triggered my gag reflex and tears. The stench reminded me of dead fish under the bright, hot sun. Another hot breath blew across my face, pushing my hair back and making me gag again. My face and hands turned opposite to feel the wall behind my back. I used them to guide me to the corner. Once there, my hands reached out to feel for whatever stalked me. My breaths turned to short bursts. Anticipation of something grabbing me sent my heart into a fast, high-pitched beat. When would the attack occur? When would it strike? How would it strike? The tension took bites out of my stomach. Would it use sharpened or dull fingernails? Would it bite me? I cried, trying to guess what it might do to me.

A loud screech erupted. I covered my ears. At least I could hear again. Or was it just in my mind? I finally heard something. No. It muffled into deafness again. Another pulsing screech not only made my head hurt, but also forced pain down my spine into my arms.

The light came on, dimly. I sighed heavily, thankful my eyesight returned along with sound. I regretted being able to hear the screeching sound that resembled a high-pitched buzzsaw. Shaking, my heart revved into high gear. I closed my eyes, afraid to see what came closer. As dim light surrounded me, I sighed, my heart slowed, and I stopped sweating.

I'm back in my room again. Thank, God.

"God's not here." The whisper made my ears cold.

"What?" I thought.

"Light's not here. The warmth of his love's not here."

It was barely audible, but I shivered at the eerie words.

"He cannot hear your prayers."

"Stop it," I thought.

"He couldn't possibly love you."

"Stop it," I thought.

"You will never see him. He hates you."

The prickly voice made the hairs in my ears cold. They tingled. The fear spread through my ear canals, to my mind, pushed down into my body, and nestled itself into my soul.

"There's no hope, here."

"Stop it. Stop it. Stop it. Stop it! Stop it! Stop it!"

A maniacal laugh erupted. It surrounded me, bounced off the walls, and wrapped around me like a blanket. Ironically, it took away what little warmth existed.

"Please, stop. Please. I don't want to be here anymore." This time, my eyes found tears. *"Who are you?"*

"I am you. You are me."

"What do you want with me?"

"I heard your father. He hated you."

"No. He loved me. I know he did."

"He thought you were a sniveling pussy."

"Stop it!"

"He is with me below but doesn't want to see you."

A reddish glow opened in front of me and widened into a large circle. Soon, it was large enough to eat my bed with me on it. I heard them: high-pitched wails, screams, low roars, and countless people begging for some sort of reprieve. Is that where I'm going?

As the circle grew, I fell inside – tumbling, screaming, reaching for anything on the side to break my fall. Confused, disoriented, I could not position myself to find anything. Spinning, the blood left my head, making me dizzy.

I landed on my bed, bouncing several times. Every bounce felt higher, and every fall seemed longer. After the mattress stopped recoiling, I remained still, transfixed at the ceiling hidden by darkness. Burning pains on my skin flared, feeling like insect stings, or perhaps as if severely burned. Strangely, a bitter cold resided in the still air.

Scaly, disgusting hands grabbed my arms. While its reeking breath invaded my nostrils, I could not see its face. Every turn of my head could not escape the stink of a dirty homeless person who had not bathed in weeks – perhaps months.

It threw me into a chair that immediately sent icy pricks into my buttocks and back. They felt like tiny iron spikes – or more like sharp nails. Immediately, heavy, cold chains wrapped around my upper toros, and my legs. The creature pulled the chains tighter, driving the nails deeper into my skin. The pain flared like lightning in a thunderstorm all over my back. The ones on the seat poked the skin on my ass and balls – feeling like jolts of popping electricity.

"Please, let me go. Please let me go. This really hurts!"

"Solve the riddle boy, before the chime strikes six and I'll loosen the chains and the steely pricks. Unable to answer, I'll take delight in your wails, as you spend the night on this chair of nails."

I tried to remember what he said. *Riddle? Riddle? What riddle?* The pain was so agonizing, it was hard to think. I tried shifting from the left to the right, and from front to back. Nothing helped. In fact, every move made the spiking and fiery pain worse. And I had to spend all night on this chair? "Okay, okay," panicked, scared – my voice strained. "What's the riddle?"

"It had so many locks that don't need a key. It was far too many for you to count. It was never to be shortened, for a vow had been said. It was a symbol of strength that flowed from the head. But in a moment of weakness, its secret was out, it lay all in pieces when she gave the shout. What is it?"

The loud bellowing chime sounded like a large bell that clanged next to my head. Unable to cover my ears, all I could do was writhe in the chains. The vibrations bounced back and forth, ebbing away. My thoughts raced. I struggled to think as those nails cut into my skin. *Locks? Don't need a key? What kind of locks don't need a key? Shit, this hurts!* It felt like a thousand red hot needles pressing my skin. Did I bleed? How could I bleed in here? This wasn't real. It was some sort of torture chamber in my mind that this thing created. My mind went back to the riddle. This thing is like Freddy Kruger – except real. Its cold presence, malevolence, torture, and terror imbedded deep within me. "It was never to be shortened, for a vow had been said, it was symbol of strength, which flowed from the head." *What? What does that mean?*

The second chime thundered, penetrating my ears deeper, trying to tear my eardrums apart. The nails dug deeper, triggering pain to swirl throughout my back and butt, preventing any thoughts of escape. They seized my thoughts and froze my mind to where I couldn't think.

A third chime struck again, so loud its vibrations almost knocked my chair over. It seemed louder than the last time. I grunted, trying to find a frame of mind to think through the answer. *Think, think, think.* My scattered thoughts found the pieces of the riddle and pulled them together. "But in a moment of weakness, its secret was out, it lay all in pieces when she gave the shout." Someone had a secret. A secret of strength. It lay in pieces after the secret was revealed. Locks?

The fourth chime struck, again pulsating through my ears and bones. My skull felt like the noise would shatter it – along with my ribs, hips, and thigh bones. Trying to lurch forward, the freezing chains pulled tighter, making the punctures worse. Unable to think, too weak to free myself, I cried out and inhaled deeply – hoping it might help me think.

The fifth chime blasted through, knocking down the walls, and leaving a crack in the floor. The time between the chimes seemed shorter. This wasn't fair! How can I think when these sharp, cold points are pressing painfully on my hide? My skin pressed tighter into the nails, sending streaks of fiery, sharp pain into my skin. Sweat poured through my palms, head, soaking my skin and my … HAIR! Locks of hair! Delilah! Samson! "I'm Samson's hair!"

The room quieted to a dead silence – except for my crying and breathing. The chains mysteriously disappeared, along with the nails. Still feeling the pinches of the tips, I dropped to the floor, and fell into a deep sleep.

I woke up. When I got out of bed, the room tilted, swiveling from left to right. What the hell? I stood in the shower as beading water dripped off, but felt different: thicker, slimy, and gross. Somewhat cold, I kept turning the heat up. The water spraying sounded weird. The noise on the shower curtain was incredibly loud whereas the echoes of water bouncing off the tile were soft and low.

Just out of the shower, I stood on the cold tile. The room stretched incredibly far. It tilted again. I almost fell. Shadows enclosed and circled me. Whispering caught my attention. Strangely, I had no control of my body. My arms lifted at the joints: my wrist, elbow, and shoulders, but it felt as if something like piano wires pulled on them. Something manipulated the wires, that also seemed connected to my knees and ankles.

Gazing at the bathroom mirror, the horrifying image shook me. Not screaming, I simply retreated to shock. Quivering, I could not believe my eyes. Sores covered my face. Some bled, others leaked puss. They hurt. Some burned, some itched, others had a very dull ache. My eyes bled – as well as my ears.

In a daze, I somehow dressed myself and went downstairs. The house tilted again, rocking from left to right, and backwards and forwards – moaning every time. Taking a tight hold on the handrail, I hoped I didn't fall going down the stairs. My knees, thighs, shins, and feet all hurt with every step.

At the table, eating breakfast, Mom and Elise stared at me while keeping their distance. The food had no taste, lacking the sweetness of sugar or the tartness of salt. My arms hurt at every joint – even my fingers. Confused, I tried to talk to them, but they sounded like sped up conversations on a recorder that put the voices in a higher pitch. A minute later, their voices distorted and folded on themselves. I could not understand them at all. They spoke louder, as if trying to communicate better, but it remained gibberish.

"What's going on? What's happening?" I asked.

My own words had become warped and indiscernible, becoming a distortion of nonsense. Did Mom and Elise understand? Their hands, arms, and fingers shook, and their jaws quivered.

I tried to talk to them again. "What's happening?" I only heard nonsense. Is that what they heard? Their nervous eyes cast a quick glance, then shifted back to their plates. Their faces warped, as if waves of heat passed in front of them. Conversations were fast, while at other times the voices sounded slow. Either way, I couldn't understand either of them.

Abruptly I found myself watching TV. The character dialog sounded like gibberish. If I didn't know the show and some of its lines, I would have had no idea what they said. Strangely, even thinking about the funniest lines, I felt no laughter – and could not even find a smile. Some sad scenes that usually made me cry had no effect. The emotions bounced off my heart, keeping me from any empathy, joviality, and peace. It felt like I constantly shook without moving, and my fingers, hands, toes, and legs shook so hard in fear, they froze. Puzzled, in a daze, I stared ahead, remaining still and silent.

Time became rapid, pushing me along at breakneck speed. Showering, eating, watching TV. Out of the light, into the dark. Screaming. Horrible faces. Loud noises. Indiscernible talk. The routine repeated. It happened again – only faster. It felt like someone hit the fast-forward button – affecting my whole life. The sounds, conversations, music, and studio audience laughter all sounded distorted – laced with something evil and unsettling.

Elise led me up the steps. They went on forever. She glanced back, but quick enough as not to receive my angry stare. Why was I staring at her like that? The staircase tilted to the left as the floor moaned and creaked, then they swiveled to the right. Feeling as if I would fall, I took a tight hold of the railing, as well as Elise's hand. She recoiled. I felt the chill in her skin, and possibly her person.

I counted the steps. Up to 40, I wondered when I'd get to the top. Did I want to? It was pitch dark above me. I couldn't see the end of the steps. After what seemed like ten or twenty minutes of climbing, we reached the top. To the left, the landing was swallowed by a cold, cavernous darkness.

Elise turned to me. Her lips quivered. The blood drained from her face. She hugged me – but quickly. She said something that drowned in loud thuds. I could not make it out as I dropped into a long, drawn-out, deep yawn. Her shaking fingers clasped the doorknob, struggling to turn it. Elise left the room and shut the door fast – leaving me in the dark.

My room, freezing, made my skin quiver. It felt like tiny bits of insects crawled on my skin, leaving behind cold pricks. They dug into my pores, and my muscles. They even found a way to my bones. I heard more wails. I heard … organ music. It sounded wicked and terrifying. It also warped into long soundwaves, growing louder. An unholy chorus of indiscernible words accompanied the terrifying music.

The lights returned. There was Father Matthew. Sister Regina was next to him. They tried to constrain me. My arms pushed them back as if they were dolls. I slapped Sister Regina across her left cheek. I shoved Father Matthew in his chest – after knocking the Rosary Beads and the cross out of his hands. He fell into the wall, cracking it and leaving a small hole.

The image of … whatever it was … returned. The long, shadowy ears, the tall, lean arms, and legs. Slitted eyes, triangular, pointing towards the outside of the thin head. They glowed. Sometimes they were yellow, and within seconds they were red. It had no nose, but a huge gaping mouth, laced with jagged, broken, and sharpened teeth.

Scarier, though, was when I saw my own face. It terrified me with sickly, pale skin that flaked between my upper and lower lips. Burns covered my cheeks, and one of my ears looked mangled. Sweat poured from gashes, along with blood and puss.

Hurled through a dark tunnel and back into my room, I felt dizzy, nauseated, and confused. All the action figures were gone, along with my books and movie collection. I kept trying to find something that circled me but remained just beyond my vision. Spinning, I tried to find it, but it kept eluding me – almost causing me to stumble. I grabbed my desk to brace myself.

I floated in pitch black until some light tightened and formed in a window. Or was it a mirror? I saw my body on the bed. Above me was Father Matthew and his friend talking to me, but I could not understand them.

I screamed as the creature burst forth from my body. It growled and snapped at the priest while its fiery, eyes scowled at the priests and nun. They spread incense – but to me, it smelled like cow or horse shit. The creature copied my actions: recoiling at the stench and cringing at their thunderous and cacophonous prayers that hurt our ears.

The awful noise ceased once they stopped praying, and the shadowy demon pushed back into my body. But I'm out of my body? Is that right? I'm trapped out of my body that lay there like a dead corpse. I tried to return to it, but something yanked me back. Scared, frantic, I tried again to return to my body, but again something pulled (or pushed) me away. I reached and kicked, trying to meld with my body. Although that thing already dwelled inside me, I preferred its company as opposed to it expelling me into nothingness. What would happen to me if I remained free from my body for too long? Fade into nothing or cease to exist? Neither was appealing – and frightened me to the core.

The lights dimmed as the darkness contracted and swirled around me. Soon, I could not see Father Matthew or Sister Regina, but only my body that appeared lifeless. Something drew me slowly within my body. Grateful, relieved, I sighed – until the stinking breath blew across my nose as I heard the raspy breathing. The breaths shot through its nostrils, in a laughing rhythm. I closed my eyes, not wanting to see it, but the image penetrated my eyelids. Pinching my nose shut did not stop the rancid, indescribable stench.

Did I wake up in the middle of a nightmare – only to find myself in another one?

How long have I been here? A day? A week? A month? I needed something to grasp or touch to keep me grounded, but nothing existed for me to grab. A faint outline from my shuddered windows emerged. My laptop started letting the screen's light illuminate the room. My lengthened shadow draped over my bed and grew up the wall. My laptop had wallpaper of a hideous, monstrous, creature. Its sunken eyes had bugs crawling out of the sockets and its mouth had hollowed out into a deep, dark hole. High pitched screams flew out, hurting my ears like fingernails on a chalkboard.

Its arms thrust through the screen. I rushed backwards and hit the wall. The mirror on my door displayed shadowy creatures that moved back and forth, casting counter-shadows and silhouettes. They moved around like a demonic kaleidoscope and formed into an image. The light flickered and grew, subtly. Just enough illumination helped me see the image: me? It's my own dumb reflection.

The mirror image changed. My eyes grew black, my forehead tilted forward, and my reflection sneered. My reflection's arms pushed through from the inside of the mirror. The glass did not break, but rather rippled like lake water after throwing a stone in it. My image pushed through harder, first freeing its shoulders, then its head. The hands wrapped around my neck. Pressure and pain hindered breathing until I cringed as strands of flesh draped across my mouth. Within seconds, my mouth disappeared! I could not scream! How could I eat? How could I breathe?

My reflection yanked me into the mirror. No glass broke. No shards cut me or lacerated my skin. As I fully passed through, brightness filled my room, along with action figures, books, collectibles, and Minibike Competition Trophies except ... were they backwards?

Looking at the mirror from the inside terrified me. The sounds of my footsteps and breathing reverberated, magnifying not only in volume, but distortion. Light inverted on itself, growing larger in corners while shadows increased near lamps and open windows.

Turning around, I peered into the real world. Or was I in the real world looking into a false one? Feeling dizzy and nauseated, I fell to my knees and guarded my stomach. Grunting, I tried to stuff down the feeling, but my innards curled and tightened so hard, they only found one escape: up. Everything came out violently, spewing across the room – leaving a bitter, disgusting taste over my tongue. The vomit did not fall to the floor, but separated into three, four, five streams that circled into larger balls and floated.

Standing, shocked, confused, my eyes glared at the reality I left. Mom had backed into a corner with Elise. A large, inhuman shadow creature loomed over them. The deformed, long arm swung across the room, carrying books, decorations, collectibles, and school supplies with it. The room distorted, elongating in the direction of the arm. The other arm took a turn, stirring a burst of wind in the opposite direction, carrying the airborne items with it. The room contorted once again. It sprang at them, but

Mom put herself between the creature thing and Elise, trying to protect her.

The monstrous entity took ahold of her neck and lifted her off the floor. It swiped at her with the free hand. Mom's screams echoed backwards. Piercing, cringing screams twisted, stretched, and thickened. It triggered more nausea, and more vomit spewed, curled, and swiveled into misshapen, floating balls.

I pounded from the inside (or was I outside?) of the mirror, begging it to stop. My own voice warped, compressed, then spread out into circles making them dissonant. It finally let go of Mom, letting her fall to the floor, bloodied, and bruised.

It turned to face me, tilting its head. For a split second – it was Dad! It changed to a long, devilish face and eyes that reminded me of those creatures from the "Alien" movies. A thin, darkened head robbed all light. It did have slanted eyes like those of an evil Jack O Lantern that glowed a sinister orange light.

Cringing, I stared at my own body that lay on the bed in the other world. It looked dead. Does that mean I'm dead? Dizzy, I saw the image of the evil thing again, followed by my emaciated and sickly face. The image of the entity's face appeared longer every time it returned while my face lasted less and less.

Father Matthew and his friend stepped into the light and continued his rituals. The painful noise vibrated louder and louder – like the subwoofer on our home entertainment system. My ribs shook and my stomach and heart vibrated with each pulse. It seemed like each boom pushed me further away from my body.

Unnerved, I tried … swimming towards my body. I was in the air, but it felt thicker like water. I pushed and pulled but found nothing to firmly grab or push against. What would happen to me if I couldn't get back there? Float forever? Fall into nothingness? Fade from existence? Something sucked my … spirit back into my body. Both relieved and scared, I felt the slimy, disgusting demon next to me.

"You're going to die," It whispered.

"Please stop."

"You're an awful child."

"Please stop."

"Your mother blames you for all of it."

"God, please help me."

"God is not here."

"Leave me alone, please. I wanna go home with Mom and Elise. Please let me go."

It taunted me continuously. Never stopping, it insulted me, Mom, Dad, Elise, Gunner. It threatened them. It

threatened me. Its awful smell and hot breath no longer
mattered. What mattered was how I felt trapped with this
thing. The mocking continued for … I don't know how
long. Every time it spoke, the despair piled higher,
thicker, and heavier. It reminded me of the time when
Elise buried me in the sand at Martha's Vineyard.

How long have I been in this place? I had no way to
keep track of the minutes, hours, or days. It seemed like
forever. Was this a dream? It seemed like one. No, this
resembled a continuous nightmare. Why can't I wake up?

"Wake-up!"

Stuck, I tried yelling in my thoughts more.

"Wake up! Why can't I wake up? Please, wake up!"

My volume surged, hoping to stir me awake – except
my words echoed loudly, repeating four, five – maybe
even ten times. Nobody heard me from here. I was all
alone, by myself with nobody to talk to or share with –
except for the demon. Neither option seemed good. I cast
all my anguish into the words my mouth spoke. *"Wake
the fuck up! Please. I don't want to stay here."*

Was this Hell? How can I get out of here? How can I
escape? I found no options. Heavy weights pinned me,
keeping me in darkness and my heart thumped faster and
louder. Nausea, dizziness, and pains in my joints dropped
me to my knees.

Images flashed faster: the thing, Dad, me, Elise, Mom, Father Matthew, Gunner, Casey, Aunt Beth, the thing again! Me. Sister Regina. Dad. The creature. Me. Dad. The creature. Me. Dad. Gunner. Mom. Elise. Father Matthew. Me. Dad. The thing.

They all tried to talk – perhaps one word per face. Their voices exploded, distorted, slowed, and sped up – meshing into one discordant, painful sound. Am I going insane? My mind swirled with memories, images, voices, smells, and sensations that flooded so fast they confused me.

"Stop it!" I yelled. My own voice dropped, lengthened, stretched, and bounced, adding to the noises that already attacked me. "Leave me alone!" Losing frame of mind, I tried to recite one of the prayers Father Matthew taught me. Unable to say it, I shook, twitched, and panicked.

What? I sat at the kitchen table. How'd I get here? The room pivoted, stretched, then shrank as the light dimmed. My wet bangs dangled below my nose. Frozen, stiff, I felt like a cold, hardened statue with heavy, weighted bones.

Mom, quivering, held some scissors with trembling fingers. Her right eye had a gash and dry blood stained her face. Taking a deep breath, she relaxed while clipping my bangs that fell on my naked feet. Mom took a deep breath and cut some more. After a few snips, she used a towel to brush away the hair clippings off my chest and shoulders.

A frenzy exploded. As my mouth opened, incisors stretched and narrowed, pushing out a horrible pain throughout my jaw, gums, teeth, cheeks, and tongue. As my head moved forward and to the left, the thing thrust the fangs through her arm. Her scream deadened as if blocked by a thick double-paned window.

The setting instantly changed to the familiar, cold blackness – leaving me unable to see anything. I pleaded to wake up over and over. Why can't I wake up? I need to wake up. How long have I been here?

I started to forget things. Where was I? Who's that girl with the dark, raven hair and glasses? Who's the woman in the habit? What? A blind priest? Did I know him? What's his name? What's my name? Jason Michael? No. Gu … no, not Gunner. Who's Gunner? Again, trying to remember my name I guessed: Walt? Casey? Vordic? No, I'm not Vordic. I'm … I don't know. I heard it again. Vordic. "I am Vordic. I am Vordic. I am Vordic …" it repeated endlessly, going on and on, pushing and filling all corners of my mind, my heart, stomach, and spirit.

This nightmare went on and on. When will it end? When will I get out of here?

Awakening

The familiar music pulled me awake, almost triggering me to smile. Mom played "Home Sweet Home," by Motley Crue – although for some reason it seemed softer, and emptier. Was it her fingers or heart that created that particular sound? The music found my wound, somehow triggering the pain and soothing the damage at the same time.

My eyes tried to close and drag me back to sleep, but a few grunts and coughs revived me. Shit – I wish they hadn't. The physical pain pushed the inner pain down. Each breath hurt my rib cage, and every move agitated aches and pains in my skin, muscles, joints, and cartilage. I tried to sit up, but something restrained my arms.

"Mom." Weak, hoarse, my voice barely eked out a whisper. I hoped clearing my throat would ease some pain in my larynx. Although it didn't, my voice gained strength and volume. "Mom." Shit! That hurt my voice box. I grunted and belted out "Mom," once again. My sounds reached her ears as she rushed up the stairs and burst into my room.

"Jeffrey? Are you there? Are you okay?"

Mom's voice was the best thing I heard in a long time. It didn't echo, or warp into something inaudible – and I no longer heard nightmarish things like evil, unearthly wails, crying, yelling, moaning, or ominous singing. Pitch blackness no longer surrounded me, shadows didn't reach for me, and that god-awful dream had vanished. The frigid air left, too, leaving a nursing warmth that imbedded itself deep into my skin, muscles, bones, and spirit.

Images danced in my mind: faces of doctors and nurses horrified, Elise and Mom terrified, crying, and … bloodied? Did I hurt Mom and Elise? How could I do that?

Hideous, ugly faces appeared for a few seconds, exhaling putrid breaths that triggered my nausea. Although their black eyes had no hope or life, their gaping mouths and taut cheeks indicated hatred. Their cold, strong arms tried to grab me as their skin flaked. Aghast, I pulled my limbs close, terrified of what they would do.

I knew what they were: Zombies. They were the one thing that truly scared me because they never stopped, always keeping pace, never tiring. Whether it was a virus, or radiation, or even something supernatural, their numbers never dwindled, but always grew. If you found a refuge, even a well-stocked one, they would wait you out until everything was used. All the images, noises, and sick, tormented imaginations ceased.

I was back in my room! Mom appeared.

"Sweetie. Are you there?"

"Mom," I whispered, "what's happening to me?" I struggled for breath. It hurt to inhale, and more so to exhale. The discomfort spread with every gasp. My throat felt as if someone had thrown gravel and sand in it. It throbbed as I spoke. "M … Mom … I'm really scared." I cried. "I don't know what's happening to me." Although she hugged me tight, I could not return the embrace. I stammered. "Why can't I move my arms?"

"We had to … restrain you. To … keep you from hurting yourself … and us."

"I hurt you?" Seeing Mom's face, I cried more. A bruise purpled her eye, and another discolored her cheek. I recognized the gash above her right eye along with a blood stain – some of it was in her hair.

She whispered. "You didn't do it. It was … something else."

A rank stench almost made me vomit. Was that me? My neck had spasms of pain, shooting across my back under my shoulder blades and down my arm. It felt like something had stretched my bones too far, almost to the point of breaking. The pain throbbed intently. I felt so thin – much more than I already was. Was that me who smelled so bad? Hunger pangs punched me in the gut. My mouth craved moisture. "I'm so mega thirsty," my raspy voice struggled. "I need something to drink."

She cried. "That's my boy. Always saying things are 'mega.'"

Mom made my favorite: waffles, scrambled eggs, and bacon. She still seemed nervous – keeping her distance and casting cautious glances at me. Her fingers shook although they were pale compared to mine. Her face expressed exhaustion, almost seeming as if she had a few new wrinkles. The eyes, so distraught, were a mix of fear, worry, desperation, and tiredness.

Starvation compelled me to eat – but shaking hands made it hard to stab the pieces of waffles and eggs. Although I craved water more than anything else, I had trouble holding a glass of it – needing to use both hands. Breaths expelled in short bursts, almost sounding like a steady, fast drumbeat. Closing my eyes, I took deep breaths, held them, and slowly released them. Some calm found its way into my body, and some of my spirit. I returned to scarfing down food but had to stop when the food congested in my chest, causing some pain.

"Slow down, sweetie."

I nodded and looked at her. Seeing the bits of anxiety in her eyes and the quivering of her lips added to the pain in my chest. Mom flinched, wanting to reach for me, but stopped herself – even jerking her hand back.

Finally able to take a breath, I wept. "It's me, Mom. I promise. You gotta believe me – please."

She stood, and moved to the seat to my right, wrapped her arms around me, then kissed my forehead. "I love you so much," she whispered, "but you really stink." A small laugh escaped, allowing me to forge a small grin that did not last long.

Ready to eat again, I devoured what was left of the food. I ate ravenously, savoring every bit of the eggs, bacon, and waffles. The meal provided familiarity and comfort, especially since Mom made it for me.

After gulping a whole bunch of water and devouring the food, Mom helped me to the jacuzzi in her bedroom. Even my toes and feet hurt. Getting into the spa, the water was perfectly warm. Neither too hot, nor too cool, this water provided healing and soothing relief. I held my knees to my chest. Once the water was level with my shoulders, Mom put the jets on low. The warm bubbling water felt good. She used a washcloth, dabbing it with soap and cleaning my skin, arms, and head.

Normally, I'd feel humiliated sitting naked in a tub in front of Mom, but feeling so helpless, I just let her clean me. She even washed my long, stringy, and matted hair. Every joint, muscle, and limb hurt. My fingers felt as if they had been working on a motor for days on end. My breaths still pulsed, sending waves of pain in my chest, and spreading to my arms, legs, fingers, and toes. I relaxed as the warm water continued pouring into the large tub, pulsing, and healing me. I wanted to immerse myself and clean out the demon inside me. Or maybe I could drown it.

My eyelids fluttered. "Where's Elise?"

"She's with your Aunt Beth."

I hesitated, realizing Sis stayed there for safety. "Does Gunner still have his dick?"

Mom laughed … and cried at the same time. "She's okay – and so is your cousin. However, you (or rather it) gave Uncle Walt a broken arm and a dislocated shoulder."

"The … thing did something right," I muttered. The memories recalled an incident with Father Matthew and Sister Regina, but it was too vague to remember. It

solidified, helping me remember it perfectly. "Mom …
did I hurt Father Matthew? Where is he?"

Mom hesitated. "He is … petitioning the Church to
perform … an," she took a huge breath, "exorcism."

I stopped staring ahead and looked at her.

"I didn't believe it myself," she whispered, "until I …
saw … unbelievable … things."

"Like what?"

Her eyes, laced with terror, leaked tiny tears. She
whispered, but I heard everything clearly. "You … lifted
off the floor. You looked like a marionette pulled up by a
puppeteer. You clawed the walls for hours on end. You
… stood on the … ceiling upside-down. Your eyes bled.
And you … received heavy burns on your torso where
Father Matthew splashed … Holy Water on you."

I cringed. Glancing at my chest, I saw the fainted
images of burns. They formed a crude cross.

A significant memory returned. It was with Dad after
he and I saw a movie called "The Conjuring."

*"Dad – do you believe in that stuff? The supernatural?
Ghosts and demons?"*

*He smiled while hunching his shoulders. "I honestly
don't know if I do or not. Maybe it's real, but I've never
experienced anything like that. Your Aunt Janet and
Uncle Dan experienced something, but you'd have to talk*

to them. So, it might be real ... or it might just be stories used for fiction, TV, and movies. Does that stuff scare you?"

My chest thumped nervously while I thought about those things. I took a deep breath before whispering my answer: "Yes. If that stuff's real – it does scare me."

"But you know the movies and the books are fiction, right?"

I nodded. "Yeah. But the things behind them could be real."

Sitting next to me, he clasped my shoulder and pulled me closer. "I wish I could tell you for sure – but I just don't know. What you can know is that you can always rely on me and your mother to love you."

Feeling better, I smiled.

"And I think you can rely on your sister, too. Maybe."

A small laugh escaped.

Returning to the now, my heart ached for Dad to talk to me again. That pain hurt the most.

I noticed something else. "Mom, how ... long was I like that? It's like ... I'm so ... thin."

Mom paused, taking a deep breath. She was scared. Not as if seeing a good horror movie, but rather purely frightened into trauma. "Sweetie," she pushed my bangs back. "This last episode was ... almost a month long."

I bit my lip. "That thing had me for … a month?" Shocked, I stuttered as a few tears seeped through my eyelids. "And … how many … episodes have I had?"

"Three." She inhaled deeply, preparing for the news. I flinched, waiting for the shock. "The first one was for a week."

I stared ahead as my lips, my jaw, and my skin all quivered.

"Then you came back to us for five days. But then you … or rather it returned for two weeks. You came back for three days. Then, the one you just came out of … was almost a whole month."

The memories of weird experiences, bizarre sensory images, and illogical patterns … suddenly became discernible. Strange voices, darkness, trying to talk and listen to others, feeling separated from myself, trapped, a shrinking reality confused me like thousands of jigsaw puzzles that did not fit. Now all those sensations connected.

"I tried to talk to you, didn't I?"

Mom whispered a sigh. "Yes, but … we couldn't understand you – and the voice, was … well … frightening."

"Why couldn't you understand me?"

"It was … a … foreign language – at least according to Father Matthew. He said you were speaking a mixture of Latin, Aramaic, and Ancient Greek."

Perplexed, my mind tried to piece out the random elements that floated in my mind. "I couldn't hear you or Elise. Or Father Matthew." I struggled not just with talking, but also thinking. The strange memories, just out of reach, faded in and out. "Your voices sounded … muffled or … messed up. I tried to … to talk to you but it seemed like you didn't hear me at all – or even see me." I clamped my eyes shut. "I was going crazy." I cried a bit. "I still am."

Ten, twelve, perhaps twenty sobs made it impossible to talk. Coming out like dry heaves, it took what little control I had to calm down. I had to inhale deeply many times and let the breaths out slowly. "Why is this happening to me?" I didn't say it to find an answer – because I didn't expect one. I just wanted to let it out. Maybe speaking it would release all the fear, doubt, and confusion bubbling inside me.

Mom hugged me like it was the most important thing to her. Able to reach up with my left hand, I clasped her hand tightly – as if it was the most important thing for me.

"Mom, where's Father Matthew? I need him. I gotta get him to get rid of this thing. I hate it. I don't like what it's doing to me. It terrifies me. And I certainly don't want to go back into that weird nightmare where all my hearing and talking was screwed up. It's so ..." I had trouble finding a word; "horrifying." The memory of the images, sounds, smells, and sensations tried to drown me in a never-ending nightmare. "Please, don't let me go back there. It's awful. It's like being ... stuck in a dream ... or a nightmare that goes on and never stops. I'm scared continuously for hours, or days on end, but there's no way to track the time. I'm shaking and I can't escape the awful feeling of ... dread. And I can't wake up no matter how hard I try. I can't take it again. Please don't let me go back, please. Please." I hope she understood me in my sobbing.

"I'm so sorry, sweetie."

Her hug became tighter – but I didn't resist. It was the warmest I had felt in ... I don't know. I felt her tears on my shoulder. Warm and soothing, they alleviated all the darkness, the hopelessness, and coldness that surrounded me. The fear retreated, the shakiness ebbed, and the horrifying dread lifted. No longer freezing, I relished the hug.

"Jeffrey," she said, "Father Matthew said it takes time. He must go through a Bishop, then through the Vatican to confirm this. Then, they have to get a Jesuit Priest – and then they must prepare."

"Prepare? For what? I need help now! I don't wanna go through that nightmare again." My voice strained. "And what's going to happen if that thing takes over and I don't come back? What happens to me when I don't come back?" My eyes closed tightly as I shuddered at the thought. The light dimmed in my eyes and the coldness tried to return. The dread had regrouped and closed in. What would happen to my soul? Erased from existence into nothing? Forever trapped in a cold, black darkness? Feeling pain and torture? Would I be thrown into hell – experiencing the searing heat, the pain of fire and … who knows what?

Mom gently rubbed my back. "They have to fast and pray. Have faith."

"I don't think I have any more left." I hoped she understood me.

"Believe me, sweetie, you're coming back, and it will go away for good."

The doorbell startled me. Mom kissed my forehead. "I'll be right back."

I hated this. It was like when I crashed on the minibike, dislocated my shoulder, and broke my collar bone two years ago. No. What I went through now was far worse. The memories of the nightmare, though flimsy, attacked the deepest part of me. I want to straighten out reality and rid myself of all the mental and emotional strain. Exhausted, I wanted to sleep, but feared becoming locked and lost in my nightmares again. I worried about falling back into that bottomless black pit. I silently prayed to God, hoping that thing wouldn't wake up and take over again. Asking God to get rid of it, I felt a slight punch in my stomach.

Rushed steps scurried through the house towards Mom's bathroom. Father Matthew, led by Mom and Sister Regina walked in. For a change, I felt embarrassed – mostly because of Sister Regina. Already feeling vulnerable, it faded fast.

At first, they kept their distance and stared at me. Eventually, they moved closer, but with caution and fear. "Jefferey," said Father Matthew, kneeling close to me. "I'm glad you're back for now."

"Did it leave? For good. Please …"

"I don't think so."

A faint glimmer of hope faded. "But … maybe it won't return if you're here."

"Jeffrey, it attacked the sister and me."

"How'd you know it was there?" I whispered.

Sister Regina inserted herself into the conversation. "I told Father Matthew about an experience with you in the hospital, along with your mother, sister, and cousin."

"And when I visited you, I heard it," said the father.

My head turned sharply towards him. "What do you mean … you heard it? How?"

"Jeffrey, are you aware that when a person becomes blind that their other senses heighten?"

"Yes."

"My hearing has been … as you would likely put it … mega sensitive."

I wanted to grin, but hopelessness grew, burying the iota of humor and faith that remained.

"I can hear those things."

"Really?"

"And as a priest, I have another sense of things … unholy things. That, too, increased. As well as my sense of touch, which feels supernatural presences."

"Have you had a lot of those experiences?"

"Just a few."

I pondered what he said. Did he hear the same things I heard? The demonic wailing, the horrifying chorus? The deep, hoarse voice that growled? After a quiet minute, I had to tell him the one thing running around in my mind all day. "It's my fault."

"Honey," said Mom, "it's not your fault."

"Jeffrey," added Father Matthew, "…no it's not. Don't blame yourself. Everyone has doubts. This thing feeds on doubt and fear. Your fear of your father out of your life, what's going to happen to your mother and sister, and what the future holds."

"It's not that," I said, pounding the tub water. I cried some – then foolishly tried to dry my eyes with wet hands. "I think it tricked me. It made me think it was Dad," I stammered, "and I let it in. I remember that dream so well. Dad was in my room, and I hugged it and it revealed itself. But it was too late." I hoped they understood what I said under the sobs.

As my eyes closed … my spirit shrank. Sinister, yellowish eyes opened as it seemed to awaken deep within. The images of the zombies returned, and the dissonant chorus burst into loudness. I flinched as the buzzing in my head exploded.

"Jeffrey …" they all said. "What is it?"

"Oh, God! Oh, no." I whined, almost crying. "I think it's coming back."

Is it My Body?

Grogginess, dizziness, soreness, loneliness all confused me as a heavy drape of darkness covered me. Was I awake or lost in deep, heavy dreams? A dim light subtly grew, casting an eerie bluish aura that circled me. Spinning around, I could barely see the walls of my room along with my books, collectibles, posters, and action figures.

The door to the bathroom opened slowly, revealing an empty, black abyss. An icy fear froze me in place – although a part of me wanted to move forward. Dread dropped through me like a heavy, dense iron weight – leaving a lingering cold. Something cut through my feet, like rebar pushing deep into the floor. I tried to step forward. Unable to move, I tried stepping backwards, but my feet were stuck.

Two faint lights pierced through the darkness of the bathroom. They swiveled turning left, then right, as if examining me.

"Come in."

The whisper left an icy chill in my ears. Invisible restraints released me, allowing me to walk into the bathroom. The lights did not work, but a faint illumination outlined the mirror. Walking towards it, the faint lights became my reflection – but the image changed. My skin, decayed and flaking, had a grayish color, and my hair looked longer, thinned, and matted. Lips had swollen and chapped, and I gasped seeing my jagged, uneven teeth.

For a split second, it changed to a taller, menacing creature. Its eyes, flatter and yellow, looked like those of a cat – or perhaps a snake. The nose was empty, while the long mouth spread revealing its jagged teeth laced with blood and pieces of rotting meat.

Now it looked like me again. It switched every few seconds. Leaning closer, my stomach twitched with my erratic breaths that fogged the reflective glass. Its breath also spread across the mirror – freezing it from the inside.

My jaw quivered as I stared. The question burning in my mind came through my mouth. "Who are you?" The remnant of my voice bounced off the tile a few times, leaving a fading echo.

"I am you." The voice, deeper, thicker, also spread like displaced water after throwing a stone into a pond.

"I don't want you here." I stammered as uncertainty and fear dripped through my voice. "I want you to leave. Please get out of my room." Realizing the invasion was far deeper, I took a breath and made my voice stronger and blunter. "I want you to leave me. Go away."

A conniving, sinister chuckle escaped from the lips. Growing in volume and density, it spread – again chilling the hairs in my ears and my nose. It stopped and waited until the echoes became empty. *"I'm not leaving. You let me in. You invited me. And I like it here."*

The overwhelming dread and sadness triggered a few tears, then the fear let loose some more. "Dad!" I called out. Maybe his ghost could hear and help me. "Dad, are you here? I need your help." Unheard, my prayers and pleas did not escape this pit, and fell hard on my head like stones.

"He's not here," it said. *"He's in the abyss with the others. He's happy there. He's glad because he hated you. He hated your disgusting guts since you and your sister were born."*

The words, rebounding, sounded louder and blunter. It seemed like it was now bouncing inside my head.

"He was embarrassed by you and was glad to get away from you."

Biting my lip, I cried heavily. "No. He loved me. I loved him."

"God killed him – you know. He thought it best to get that sick scum away from you."

Disgusting gray hands jumped from the blackness and grabbed my shoulders, arms, knees, thighs, and waist. Long, dirty, and splintered fingernails dug into my skin and pressed hard. Falling into a ball, more of them prodded me and punctured my skin. "Stop it, please. It hurts. Please stop it."

The hands disappeared and my yells drowned in an eerie silence. The stinking, dead air pressed against me, almost making me vomit. Something brushed against my back. Scaley, rough, it barely rubbed my shoulder. Turning around, I tried to find it – but it kept eluding me and staying just beyond my eyes. "Who are you? Leave me alone."

"Let's play hide and seek. Come find me."

"No. Leave."

"Then I'll find you."

My breathing and heartbeat were so erratic and uncoordinated I could not form a plan or any response. I kept spinning to the left, then to the right to catch the thing that circled me. "Who are you?"

The presence disappeared, along with its sulfurous stench and snickering laugh. My breaths and my heart froze – locking into place. The emptiness captured me and dragged me into a panic. Unable to think of a plan, I stood like a statue.

Its image appeared in a red, sinister light. The demonic eyes, the misshapen nose, and mouth all appeared at once. The smile widened, revealing the horrid teeth that grew into sharp blades. It lunged at me, yelling. *"Run and hide if you can! I'll find you!"*

My frozen heart and breaths exploded as I burst into a run. Where was it? Behind me, beside me, or before me? A presence followed me, radiating its cold feeling and a hot breath. I ran faster when a brush of air skimmed the back of my neck, leaving behind a cold tingling that pressed the hairs on my neck and chilled my skin. I should have felt the wall by now, but instead, my head bounced a wooden door open. Splintery, I noticed a thick mucus dripping through the rough wood. Finding another door, I pushed through and discovered a small room with a dim light bulb. Another door, another room, with a brighter bulb. Another door, another room, and a brighter bulb and … Freddy!

My dog, his ears folded back, barked, growled, and snarled at me – then tried to bite my leg. How'd he become so big? Why was blood dripping from his teeth, and what was that horrid meat stuck in his mouth?

Running, I burst through another door. The … whatever it was appeared and grabbed me.

"Caught you! I win!"

It lifted me up and laughed in my face, spreading its slobber, stink, and terror all through me. I was back in my room – with Father Matthew, Sister Regina, and another priest surrounding me, and they all spoke a weird language. It hurt my ears, pounding both within and outside my head. Spinning around, I realized the room seemed darker and smaller.

A reddish hue enveloped me. Only a spectator, the only thing I could do was watch, and go along. I kept fading in and out of consciousness, every time finding less of myself and more of something else. The images of Mom, Elise, Dad, and Gunner kept flashing in my mind. Every time, they faded faster. They moved further away until disappearing. Spinning, I became dizzy, losing myself and finding more hate, fear, and dread. Where was I? Who am I?

My faith wobbled as darkness encroached. Anxiety bubbled. My skin tingled. Joints, fingers, and toes shook. Confusion set in. What was going on? Hearing voices, I tried to make them out – but like before they muffled and changed. Unable to hear their words clearly, I yelled out for someone to help. As I did, the words echoed back, hurting my ears. The high-pitched noise felt like an ice pick stabbing my brain.

A dark shadow passed over. What light radiated outlined the creature. A bright light flashed, revealing its full image: tall, long legs, gray in color, and covered in scars. A thick secretion oozed from the skin. It stank heavily. Sores splotched the torso and dripped blood. A couple of slits let intestines seep. The stomach and chest lifted and expanded with each breath. The arms, also long and sinewy, still had taut and fibrous muscles. At the end were misshapen hands that only had three clawed fingers. The shoulders had spear-like points. The lean neck stretched as veins just under the skin pulsed. Its head, long, thin, had two large, black, sunken eyes. Flies and gnats flew from the sockets. Blood and some other substance dripped. The mouth had jagged, broken, and missing teeth. The mouth widened, revealing a sinister smile. I heard a breath escape, as well as the fine mist accompanied by the vile smell. It scoffed, only letting out air. The low hissing and stuttering sound resembled a sinister laugh.

Please, let me go. Please, let me go. The thought repeated endlessly. Quivering, crying, I whispered my request, then said it louder. God how I hated this thing that encroached in my home, in my room, and … is it in me? "Who are you?"

A burst of light wrapped around it. I cringed at its vile scream. The ice pick jabbed at my brain again. No, not a real ice pick, but it felt like one. It screamed more as I heard weird voices. Was it another language, or more words retreating backwards? They echoed loudly, competing with the creature. The voices got louder. Although I couldn't hear them well, a huge breath blew out my lungs. It forced me to speak.

"Vordic!" I repeated it twice, although I did not recognize my own voice. My lungs and voice box, pushed to the limits, forced me to cough painfully. I held my chest and guarded my throat.

It burned! What was that burning on my face, my forehead, and now my chest? "Stop it!" I yelled it over and over as the burning seared my skin, muscle, and bone. I convulsed.

The thing screeched as if it endured heavy pain. It fell to its knees and howled in agony. The thunderous noise exploded in my head. Covering my ears just made it worse. Those noises mixed with my yells into a frightening wail.

The blinding light returned. It felt comforting, warm, and peaceful. It disappeared – allowing the cold to return, feeling more frigid than before. The stench that vanished also returned, triggering my gag reflex. The demon grabbed me by the arm, lifted me up and slapped my face. The fiery pain felt like wasp stings in my face. It spread to my gums and tongue.

The powerful light returned again. Although blinded, at least I got a reprieve from the pain, the cold, and the nauseous smell. Yet, as the creature grabbed both my arms, it stretched them as far apart as it could. My shoulders and elbows, pulled to maximum levels, felt as if they might break, and my wrists burned like nothing else. The fire would not go away. "Let me go, please." My voice drowned in its own sobs.

It hit me across the face three times. With every blow, the stinging pain in my mouth and face flared. It felt like stingers stuck in my skin and tongue, injecting painful venom. Also with every blow, I caught glimpses of the huge light again. Even with eyes fully shut, the light got through. Three figures, faintly silhouetted within it.

Three more hits. More pain. More flashes of light. I saw the figures again. I heard the strange, backwards voices again. They got louder. Three more hits. Three more flashes. Three – now four silhouetted figures. One reached at me, grabbed me by my shoulders and pulled.

The creature tightened its grip on my hand as something yanked it up. Pulling me close to its body, I recoiled at the feeling of its veins pulsing against my body, along with its disgusting sweat. It burned. My ears felt as if they would burst at any second. The ugly demon seized me by my neck. I desperately inhaled but found nothing. My chest heaved, trying to pull in something to breathe. It threw me to the ground. Painful coughs expelled the carbon dioxide, allowing me to find something to breathe. Now it grabbed me by the wrists again and pulled my arms and joints to the max. Was it pulling me apart? Panicked, unable to think, I twisted, fought, and tried to wriggle free.

For a split second, light flooded in. I saw the three – no four figures within the light. A sweet pleasing aroma refreshed my spirit as a comforting warmth surrounded my body like a hot bath. The awful dread retreated, as well as the agonizing pain. Almost fully inside the light, I tried to crawl into it, but nothing solid existed to provide an anchor for either pushing or pulling my way into it.

The creature grabbed me again and pulled tight. Light faded, darkness wrapped around, the frigid air followed with a vile stink. The thing held onto me as we fell onto the cold, concrete floor. All the air left my body. I coughed, trying to get the air back. I cringed as its veins pulsed through its skin onto mine. It laughed.

The inside of my body, perhaps my soul, cried when something snatched me from that light that felt so wonderful. The deep dread returned like a punch in the face. Yanked back to the cold, dingy, and colorless cell, my mind raced for any idea. How could I get free? I kept thinking of that light and how wonderful it felt. I wanted to get back to it so much. Anything would be better than this place.

Reeking water fell on me and within a minute, it drenched my hair – leaving a cold blanket on my head. The water also hit my shoulders hard. The thick, gross water slid down my neck, back, and arms. I kept my mouth closed, not wanting any of it in my mouth. I backed away from the cold, thick drops. Looking up, I saw the water drip through some sort of grate. A dim light outlined the streams that resembled rain.

My bare feet sensed the numbing pinch of cold and rough concrete. Some feeling in my soles faded. The water had deepened a half inch or so. I backed away, hoping for a slight increase in elevation. Cold, I shivered. My body folded on itself. I tried to use my arms to warm my body, but being naked, it didn't work. Coarse freezing concrete rubbed my shoulders, back, and butt. The warmth in my skin left first. Now, my muscles twitched as they submitted to the oppressive cold. At first, I wished for a blanket, only realizing the icy water would dampen it completely within a few minutes.

Shocked, I realized the water crept up more. Over my toes, it now circled my ankles. The water rose more, and my heart sped up. Whether it was from the cold or the terror – I had no idea. All I knew was the water would drown me. Or would it freeze me to death?

I looked up at the grate and saw it again. It hovered above, looking down. Its red eyes glowed subtly. It knew drowning scared me the most. The memory exploded. I fell in a frozen pond. The water, so cold, hurt and sent me into a panic. A prisoner to the icy water, the current yanked me spitefully. It wanted to hurt me. To freeze me. To invade my lungs and stop my breathing. Trapped under the ice, I could not break free. How was I going to break out?

Dad plunged through the ice, grabbed me, and held me tight. Hoisting my head above the water, I coughed. Our misty breaths mixed and froze into tiny crystals. Mom stretched out on the ice, grabbed my arm, and pulled me to shore. She then rescued Dad, too. So cold, all my body did was shiver almost into a frozen statue.

The memory passed, but this reality (if it was reality) was no better. No current existed now – just the bitter cold. The water crept up to my calves and continued to crawl up to my knees, forcing my entire body to shake. I wondered if my tears might freeze. I looked up at the creature again. "Please, let me go. Please?" The thing above laughed. "I just want to go home. I just wanna go home and be with my mom and sister. Please. Let me go home."

Stolen Prayer

The freezing cold had gone. Wrapped in warmth, I sighed and pulled the refreshing sheets and blanket tighter. Feeling safe, I opened my eyelids, then batted them a few times to straighten the blurriness.

My head turned towards the sound of mumbling. Father Matthew had his head lowered as he prayed. So glad to see him, I partially smiled, then whispered. "Father Matthew? Is it gone?"

His head turned. His eyes bulged, receded, and sank into his black sockets. His skin grayed, shriveled, and wrinkled. The mouth opened wide, having fangs like a wolf. I recoiled at the breath that smelled like rotting meat. The terror jerked my shoulders, arms, legs then sent a scream through my lungs.

The shudders in my room slammed shut, blocking the light. Light bulbs flickered and fizzled out, and a couple exploded. The demon creature stood with a reddish glow surrounding it. Dark wings spread then flapped, creating a slight breeze that pushed my hair back and lifting the creature off the ground.

The flight carried a frigid air along with a horrid stench that made my stomach and lungs recoil. With nothing in my belly to expel, I heaved again. The skin on my chest burned, even stinging my nipples from the inside. It pushed huge beads of sweat through my pores. Every expulsion from my stomach caused more pain and perspiration. Now my tongue burned! Fiery, it was like coffee burning my mouth – or possibly biting into the hot pepper Elise snuck into my mashed potatoes.

I ran to the door – but it slammed shut in front of me. I frantically yanked on the knob while yelling. "Mom! Mom! Father Matthew! Sis! Someone! Please, help me!" I fell to the floor, still hitting the door although they had weakened to impotent slaps. Out of strength, hope, and ideas, I cried while leaning against the wall "God, why are you doing this to me?" The empty dead silence poked me, feeling like an insult from God.

My ears caught a faint sound. No – it was music. Where did it come from? Who played it? What song was it? Familiar, yet the song's title was elusive. The door in front of me opened slowly, emanating a small creak that seemed tired and frightened. Open, it led to another door, which turned inwards to a blacker darkness. Nervous, tense thumps bounced in my chest. Should I go into the darker corridor? What if this was a trick and a trap the demon set for me?

The music resonated a little louder and enticed my ears with the pleasant melody of a piano. The volume increased – filling the empty dread with some hope and life. Although cold, my instinct suggested the music gave me some sort of clue. My hands pierced the darkness, searching for a wall to guide me through the pitch blackness. The music became louder and then ... I recognized it: "Home Sweet Home." The familiar song pushed back the terror.

A warm tear streamed from my left eye. Biting my lip, I realized Mom played it. Taking a deep breath, I continued – even though the cold, rough, stone floor numbed my feet. A faint light flickered, suggesting it was some sort of beacon like a lighthouse. Not very bright, it outlined a small window. Was that a way to escape? The music stopped. I knew this was some sort of nightmare conjured by the demon, but I'll try anything to get out of this place. Placing my hands on the sill, I pulled myself, starting to go through it.

A head jumped at me. As I reeled backwards, the thing grabbed my wrist and held tight. Frightened, I screamed and tried to pull away, but the touch felt friendly, reassuring, and helpful. The peace spread from its hands to my arms, chest, and feet. White, hooded, the image was not prominent, but it was present, fading and returning a subtle glow.

"Jeffrey."

I heard it in my head. Quickly, its free hand lifted its index finger vertically over its lips, shushing me. It whispered in a foreign language. The … whatever it was … let go and I backed up, still confused.

A flickering light on the floor garnered my curiosity and attention. Next to it rested a book that seemed to beckon me to read it. Opening it, I felt a pleasant warmth, as if that small fire provided a tiny bit of hope. I held the candle close to see and read it, but the words were foreign and cryptic, making it impossible to read. Wincing, the little hope I found wasted to nothing.

Some candle wax dripped onto the paper, instantly lighting it afire. Strangely, the flames surrounded the lettering quickly died. I gasped, realizing the words changed form and … I could read it. "Hold on for just a little longer. He is coming to help, but he must be careful so Vordic will not kill you in the struggle. He's strong and has killed many, preying on those who lost loved ones."

The word rekindled my anticipation of leaving this place, and getting rid of this thing that tortured me.

Looking up at the white being, I nodded. "Hurry, please," I whispered. It nodded back.

All hope retreated as the demon emerged behind the white being (an angel?). Vordic ripped something off the angel's back, then sneered and laughed while ripping off its arm. The friendly spirit wailed in agony, but they faded into nothingness as the demon slung it away.

Vordic moved closer, sneered, and snorted – blasting slobber across my face. A few drops found their way into my mouth, leaving a disgusting and bitter taste lingering on my tongue. Thick mucus dripped from its nostrils onto my skin – leaving a burning sensation that felt like wasp stings.

A fire erupted on the stone wall before me, spreading from right to left, leaving behind a charred lettering. Unable to understand it, I squinted hoping to find some sort of clue. Latin! I knew some Latin since I was an Altar Boy.

"Read it as fast as you can."

The voice bounced in and out of being audible.

"The riddle separates the boy from the man."

"What?" I asked.

"The chimes will strike hard only six times, and if the puzzle is not solved, you're branded as mine."

I tried to read the riddle, but the terror and pressure froze my mind, then stirred it into a panic of random, super-quick thoughts. Unable to think, I took a few deep breaths to calm my mind.

My head almost burst as the first chime struck – which cracked the stone walls around me. The deep, bass ring kept pounding hard, almost knocking me down. Taking another breath, I tried to calm myself, but fear of the next loud chime had me quivering … and too tense to think. I tried to take control with another long breath and fixated on the Latin. "I am one of five."

The second chime rattled me, too, almost causing me to stumble. The vibrations knocked loose some stones, stirring dust. Again, a few deep breaths helped me recuperate. "He who receives … me will … will …" I gulped, hoping to suck the fear away from my mind. "He who receives me will …" what was that word? "Perish!" Got it. I repeated it to myself. "I am one of five. He who receives me will perish."

The third chime burst knocking me backwards and causing the wall to start crumbling. The coarse rocky stones scraped, cut, and bruised my skin. Desperate, shaking, scared, I cried for several seconds. No! I stopped and tried to think. Maybe if I closed my eyes and took a few deep breaths.

The fourth chime caused more stones to fall from the wall, breaking my concentration. Still frenzied, I focused on the writing again, hoping to find a frame of mind. "He who sent me will … will … become! He who sent me will become …"

The fifth chime rang, this time sending dust into my eyes, nose, and mouth. I coughed, then batted my eyelids to get the dust out. One more chime? Shit. I struggled to remember but repeated the whole thing one more time: "I am one of five. He who receives me will perish. He who sent me will become …" what was that last word? I couldn't think. What was that word?

Frantic tears were leaking from my eyes … wait! King! I repeated it to myself "I am one of five. He who receives me will perish. He who sent me will become king. Who am I?" Five? Five what? Who receives the one? Who becomes king? Clamping my eyes shut, I tried to sift through all the swirling thoughts, hoping to find the right one before the sixth chime. *Five – stones! Yes. A stone was received by Goliath, and I became king. It was King …*

The sixth chime fell as King David entered my thoughts. My eardrums felt as if they ruptured and bled. The five stones he gathered that brought down Goliath, then David became king of Israel.

"Too late" it whispered. "Too late. Now – you are mine!"

Words twisted, warped, lengthened, and shorted again. The yells I uttered sounded demonic. The room shifted, leaning to the left. It tilted more, almost making me fall. The room shrank.

Vordic stared into my eyes deeply, tilting its forehead closer. His stinking breath blew in my face, triggering my gag reflex. Its eyes glowed red, then yellow then red. It pressed forward some more, with my nose almost touching its scarred, dried, and flaking skin. My heartbeat raced so fast, it felt like the steady rhythm of a fast train.

Images flashed: Vordic, Mom, Sister Regina, Father Matthew, Gunner. My room, the shed, Mr. Owl, my minibike, Aunt Beth, Dad, and Elise. Their images swirled, circling me as their mumbled words shot fast, mixing into a dissonant message. I tightened my eyelids, somehow hoping to blot out the images … as well as the sounds. Dizzy, nauseous, confused, I could not distinguish my own memories and dreams.

The images of Mom, Elise, Dad, Father Matthew, and Gunner flashed so fast, they merged into a single image. The outline of the face became distinct, but the outline bounced like the sight of an old film out of its sprockets. It cleared and the familiar, sinister eyes, monstrous mouth glared at me with fury. It screamed, then wrapped its hands around my neck.

For a second, perhaps less, I found myself in that light again. It felt so pleasant and satisfying that I tried to grab something to stay within it. While there, I stole a breath and a prayer, hoping both might help me. Blackness returned, stealing the prayer back, robbing my hope. Not only could I not breathe in, but I also could not breathe out. Muffled coughs, tasting like sand and dirt, sent burning streams of pain down my chest.

The light returned and the strong, yet gentle hands clasped my legs and tried to pull me deeper into the light. The dark came back, robbing the warmth and peace, and returning me to the grip of Vordic. I felt my face turning red as I tried to take a breath.

Light. Dark. Light. Dark. It felt like a merry-go-round that alternated between the pitch black and the pleasant light. Soon, the ride no longer became light but only spun in darkness. Falling to the floor, I coughed, huffed, and desperately sucked in the largest breaths I could.

Rolling on my back, terror exploded in my chest — even jarring my ribs and sternum. The ceiling fell, bringing a frigid, bubbling air with it. My skin shivered and cringed as the cold burrowed inside. It seemed malevolent and spiteful as the cold surrounded me and attacked my body. I yanked my hands and feet closer and curled into the fetal position.

The empty cold struck harder and deeper. My insides felt like ice that expanded into my tendons, bones, muscles, and skin. Joints pulled tightly, rendering me a misshapen statue. My mind, horrified, also froze into a tight block of ice. Freezing from the inside out? Is that what was happening? "Please stop! It hurts! It hurts!" My scratchy voice strained.

The creeping cold continued to consume me, venturing up to my neck. My ears froze, then it spread into my brain behind my eyes. My tongue, gumline, and teeth all flared with an icy, numbing pain. Consciousness faded and my eyes darkened.

In pitch darkness, I found no existence – at least not in any specific place. I could think, but I had no physical body. I could not touch, or see, or hear anything in this black void. I could not see my hands – even though they were in front of me.

I nodded off but woke up almost instantly, even though I sensed a significant amount of time had passed. An eerie, empty silence surrounded me. Where is this place? What is this place? Why am I in this place? My eyes closed and I slept in the void again, feeling as if a more considerable time had passed.

Distorted images, probably memories of people, places, and events, flung far away, disappearing into the blackness. What were those memories of? Who were those people? When did those events happen? Who am I? I thought I knew. It seemed to be on the tip of my tongue, or just out of reach in my mind.

At incredible speed, the void yanked me back into … reality? There, I trembled as a hateful, vicious, and strong presence had me in its grip. I was in a room, but it existed in a hazy, red hue. A searing heat attacked my skin, burning it – much like a vicious sunburn. How could that happen without a body? My arms grew, both in length and muscle. Significantly taller, I looked down on my prey: Two priests and a nun. Who were they? A hatred swelled inside, wanting to kill them all. I let loose a huge roar, letting out a hot wind that knocked them over.

Escape

It was difficult to tell where I started, and where the demon began. Our minds kept swapping back and forth. When I had a second or two of my identity, I tried to remember who I was and where I was. Too fast! The ugly, hate-filled, and deranged mind returned, causing the lights to dim and my vision to tint red. It pushed me aside and … somehow had me back in my room? Back on the chair of nails, I cringed as the points punctured my back, my buttocks, and arms. It wrapped heavy chains around me, keeping me on the cold, sharp points.

Back in its … or our mind … it roared through my voice. A fiery pain erupted on my tongue, the roof of my mouth, and the inside of my cheeks. My mind panicked again, wanting the control back. I struggled. It kept digging into my being. At this point, I was only a spectator – nothing else. At the same time, who am I? I tried to think, but the creature occupied most of my mind. Confused, I swirled endlessly – at least that's what it felt like. The spinning hurled images of people further away.

They faded into black. Even my thoughts, will, and soul flew apart.

What was going to happen? Am I trapped in its head now? Or was he taking control of my identity? How can we both exist here at this moment? How could we both occupy the same space?

I saw some familiar faces, but unable to connect their names, my thoughts faded. Something pulled them away from me. Where did they go? Where was I going? Again – who am I?

"Vordic!" My (or rather its) voice let loose slobber and a violent, stinking wind that knocked the priests and nun down. Their names eluded me – although some remnants lay just beyond my reach.

Back in my room, I saw nothing. I felt nothing except the pain from those sharp metal nails poking my skin. The chains lifted as something pulled them away. No – not Vordic, but something else.

Back in … our mind … memories of my past warped, twisted, tilted, and swirled. I could not connect them to any name or event. When did that concert happen? What about this lake trip? Who were those old people? The girl with the thin arms, dark hair and glasses was familiar – but I could not think of her name. I struggled to remember mine. What was my name?

"Vordic!" I yelled again. That was the only thing I understood.

Back in its mind, I weakened from its violent rage. Wanting it to leave, I tried to push, but it was too strong.

The two priests spoke in a weird way as their voices slowed, twisted, and sounded like something garbled on an old AM radio. They moved slow – like zombies. The room titled, then swirled, making me dizzy.

Trapped, unable to think, all I could do was watch its view from my eyes. It launched Sister ... whoever ... and threw her into the wall. My body spun upside-down, and my feet landed on the ceiling. My hands – now covered in sores – grabbed the book out of the older priest's hands and ripped out the pages. They fluttered in a vicious gust that exploded from my nose. What did I say? I could not understand my own words that also slowed and contorted.

No more memories fired. They faded into a fine dust that smelled like sulfur. Was I going to fade, too? No. I wanted to experience ... things. What things? Things on ... Earth. What were those things? All the memories of what I tasted, touched, smelled, and viewed darkened and crumpled like paper in a fire.

The chains were off my body. Friendly hands stood me up and helped me walk.

Back with the creature, I felt all its misery fuse with my mind – leaving nothing but hatred, fear, and despair. Unable to move, act, touch, listen, or even think – I felt totally trapped, as if it sealed me inside a cast iron box and dropped in the middle of the Pacific Ocean to its deepest depths. It left me in the deep darkness without anything – even hope.

I was with the … angels … again. Is that what they were? They had to be. One of them let loose a noise that resembled a trumpet blare. Its blast expanded so fast and loud, yet I did not cringe. Instantly, the light returned, surrounding me, and they started flying me up the tunnel.

A horrid darkness reached up, engulfed me, and drug me back below into the abyss. Something strong, cold, and disgusting grabbed me, holding me tight. The stinking and flaking skin nauseated me, causing me to heave. Something punched me in the stomach. A cold, sharp, and jagged … something … pierced my essence. I convulsed as a shovel scooped out a huge part of me. The torrent of pain expanded from my chest to my limbs. The shovel dug out more of my soul and cast it aside like garbage.

A loud voice burst in my head. "Vordic." No, my name is … "Vordic!" The hideous voice – raspy, hateful – exploded in my … our head. I wanted to cover my …

our ears as it echoed. Every reverberation increased in volume.

Something wet and hot hit me. The red, hazy view of the world had a green Moon, a purplish Sun, and a sinister yellow in the stars. The trees outside my room shriveled and died. Weird, blue lightning scattered across the sky. We swiped our left hand, blowing out a window and causing debris to fly across the room. Our arms, legs, knees, hands all flared with a numbing pain.

"You watch," its sinister, hoarse voice surrounded me. "First, I will kill them and take their souls with me. I will rape your mother and sister, I will turn your cousin inside-out, and rip the flesh off your aunt slowly. I will take your father's soul with me to Sheol, the Pit, Hell – whatever you want to call it. They will suffer for all eternity, as many of my brothers do, and as I will. We suffer with horrid pain, fear, and hate. I wish it on you and your family, and all people of this world. I will take as many as I can with me into the deep bowels that separate us from the Light."

The deep gravelly voice terrified me, jabbing my spirit with nothing but dread and fear. My soul, almost completely hollowed out, was only left with a pulsing cold that spread, numbing my insides.

The light exploded again. The other spirits strongly held my legs and hips, trying to pull me deeper into the light. Vordic held onto my chest, bellowing numerous times. The ones below me bleated higher sounds. In a tug of war, I yelled. "Just let me go and die. I want to die."

Our hand slapped the younger priest, knocking him back a few feet. He shook his head, wiped the blood off his nose, and stood. Holding his crucifix high made us curl into a tight ball. The pain flared throughout our body. Legs, arms, feet, hands, all had a crushing, violent pain shooting through them. At some points, it felt like fire. A second later, they'd be freezing cold.

The two priests kept repeating something, but what? A demonic chorus sounded, rising in pitch that stabbed me with a cold ice pick in our head. We cringed – covering our ears, but the noise continued. It drowned out the words of the two holy men – that we hated with all the anger and fear within. Although we could not understand the words, they made us recoil and double up. We reeked of pain and our roar softened. The room stopped circling and leveled out. We convulsed as the priests threw more hot water.

For a split second, the water felt warm and soothing. At the same time, I straightened. Something yanked me from the thing. Finding my own identity surrounded by a light, I tried to remember who I was. Confused, panicked, I could not sort the memories. My name was … was … it was just beyond my comprehension and reach. Jeffrey! My name is Jeffrey!

The creature separated from me! It bellowed while trying to get back inside. No! I don't want it in me again. I won't let it. What could I do?

"Our Father, who art in heaven …"

The demon bellowed. Its talon poked through my tongue, making it convulse and burn. Its hands pressed tightly, and talons dug into my body, pulling itself closer, trying again to burrow back inside me.

Back in the tunnel, Vordic had lost some of its grip. The angels pulled strongly, but their clasp weakened. The light retreated while the darkness washed over me like pool or lake water. Unable to see anything, the pain returned as the creature let out snorts that sounded like laughter. It held me tighter, trying to dominate the struggle.

Back with its mind, I heard slow, muffled, and confusing words from the priests. They felt like punches to my gut, so we fought back, pushing, kicking, and knocking them over. Their images turned and twisted, disfiguring their faces.

My mind went back and forth, seeing the faces of so many people. They looked familiar, but I did not know their names. Now their facial features deteriorated into hideous images. Their eyes whitened. Their skin crinkled, folding on itself, their teeth took on misshapen forms, and the skin on their noses flew away in small bits like the nose of the Sphinx. They talked, but it was too fast and muzzled to understand. Sores and blisters formed on their cheeks and jaws. Swarms of bugs flew out of their mouths. Looking like zombies – they tried to grab me.

I screamed – although its sound lengthened, softened, and echoed. The eerie noise lifted high in pitch. My skin burned. Slits cut across my arms, my legs, torso, hands, and feet. Did my eyes bleed? Unable to see, I tried to wipe the thickened blood from my face. My existence faded – feeling as if something broke me into fine dusty particles that spread in the breeze. In a split second, I saw through the demon's eyes again as it stared through the red haze that surrounded the priests and nun.

Hurled out of my body, the light returned, this time surrounding my head, shoulders, and chest. The nice spirits held me strong and lifted me as their wings flapped. I felt one hit my head a few times.

Darkness lurched up and another creature – probably Vordic – grabbed onto my waist, trying to pull me back into that abyss. The angels screeched at him as they flapped harder. I heard the trumpet blare again. Vordic's grip loosened. It dug into my skin to cling tightly.

My heart thumped so fast; I could hear it in my ears. The continual contractions sent a fiery pain through my chest, stomach, and limbs. The demon's grip pulled me deeper into the darkness, but the angels refused to let go, barely keeping my head in the light. They screeched again, as if calling for someone. My body stretched thin, as the dull, achy pain spread from my limbs towards my heart and stomach. They both knotted. My screams filled the void, but not nearly as loud as the creatures who fought over me.

The darkness crept slowly. What little warmth I had disappeared. The light faded fast. I wanted to die. "Stop it!" I yelled. "Just let me go. Please. I want to die. I want to …"

Someone else came into the darkness. It spoke loudly. "Release this body! You are condemned to Hell." That's not what I heard in my ears. It sounded like nonsense, but somehow, I understood what it said in my mind – or perhaps my spirit. Instantly, the claws released me. Its bellow broke apart fast as it sank below me. Instantly the warm, soothing light surrounded me. The three helpers lifted me. The new entity placed its hand on my head, and

I felt a new surge of energy erupt. It felt so wonderful, spreading through my skin, chest, limbs – and into my soul. The fear, dread, and pain all scattered into tiny bits of dust.

"I am with you. You are righteous forever in my love."

Again, what I heard in my ears and mind were different. This time, the voice was peaceful and loving.

I fell hard to the floor, feeling all the pain in my joints, muscles, and bones to no end. Every breath made my rib cage and sternum ache, and my voice hurt from every cough. Sweat drenched my hair and skin, but my parched tongue felt like sandpaper. After a few grunts, I let loose a huge sigh – then I rolled on my side and coughed several times – causing the familiar pain to surge again. I started sobbing, adding to the miserably aching pain that spread in every sector of my body. Someone hugged me.

"Jeffrey! Jeffrey. Can you hear me?"

The pain prevented me from returning the affection. "Father Matthew," my weak, scratchy voice struggled between my sobs, "please tell me it's gone. Please."

"It should be gone forever," he whispered. He cried and kissed me on the forehead.

Father Bradley prayed in Latin, and I understood everything he said. "We thank you, Jesus, who, when God is in his nature, did not consider equality with God, that we must use him; but he made himself nothing, assuming the very nature of a servant, being made in the likeness of men. He humbled himself by becoming obedient to the point of death, the death of the cross. Amen."

"You priests pray mega-weird," I muttered. "Why can't you pray in English like everyone else?"

Father Matthew, still weeping, chuckled. "I'm so glad you're back with us, Jeffrey. I thought we were going to lose you. I love you."

Ignoring the pain, I latched onto him. Refusing to let go, I pulled him as close as I could while sobbing on his shoulder. "Don't let me go."

"I won't. I won't. I promise."

A refreshing healing peace settled within me – working through my entire body. The confusion and darkness ebbed, replaced with peace and light. Tension remained, but yielded to love, faith, and serenity. Warmth found its way to my chest and slowly expanded through my body. It was gone. No voices, no annoying ringing in my ears, no headache, or bitter coldness. Feeling safe, I smiled.

"Where's Mom?"

He's Back

Weak and tired, I kept grunting and coughing. Although the coughs hurt my lungs, rib cage, and throat, every new breath gave me warmth and peace – pushing the fear and dread away. Replenished, I savored every breath, drawing each one deeper into my chest. Feeling so weak and thin, my skeleton tried to poke through my skin. My parched mouth, feeling like sandpaper, craved moisture. Usually, my favorite soda was Pepsi – but I wanted water so much.

So weak, still frightened, I held onto Father Matthew tightly. He shared the embrace and kissed me on the forehead. "I'm so glad we have you back," he whispered repeatedly. "I'd love to have a son just like you." Those words wrapped around the wound of Dad's death, leaving behind ointments, bandages, and healing. "I love you."

"I love you, too," I muttered.

"Jeffrey?"

Looking over Father Matthew's shoulder, I gasped, seeing Mom for the first time since … I don't remember. She smiled as tears welled up at the bottom of her eyes, just like mine. My shoulders, elbows, and hands ached, but I did not care, holding onto Mom as tight as I could. I never wanted to separate from her again. Her grip tightened, but it didn't hurt. Instead, it was the most warm, comfortable, and secure hug.

"Sweetie," she cried, "I thought I was going to lose you. Please don't ever leave again."

The memories of the freezing cold, the dread, and the horrible fear dwindled. Sighing, I inhaled all the faith, love, and goodness in the room – unable to get enough of them. While they were alien to me, they became familiar again within a matter of seconds. The absence of those good things made me appreciate them more as I continued to breathe them in. They provided life, comfort, and refreshed my soul. I could not stop hugging Mom, and she never let go of me. "I mega love you so much, sweetie … but you stink and really need a bath and a haircut."

I chuckled, until I felt hunger pangs in my belly. "I'm so hungry."

She cradled my head in her hands. "What do you want for your meal?"

My scratchy voice struggled. "Waffles, scrambled eggs, bacon, and orange juice."

She smiled and laughed through her nose. "I should've known."

"Hey, kiddo. Your smell has improved."

Seeing Elise, I smiled amidst weeping. For the first time, I saw a whole smile stretched across her face as her eyes lit up and released some happy tears. They pushed away the Wednesday Addams persona, giving me a real sister. The strength of those skinny arms surprised me when they wrapped around my torso.

"I missed you so much," she said.

I muttered. "I can't believe you're crying."

"I'm not crying," she said, "you're crying."

I giggled. "I missed you so much. I'm so sorry for hurting you." I repeated my apology numerous times.

"I know you are." she said in a more normal voice.

I grinned. Elise continued to smile back. It was strange to see her lips stretch fully, but I liked it. "Sis, you look so much better smiling."

Her smile vanished as she returned to character. "Please don't insult me."

Going Home

Despite the rumbling hunger, the jacuzzi bath felt so relaxing. The warm waters covered me to my neck, and the bubbling water eased the pain, tension, and removed all the miry doubt swirling through my head. After soaking for 30 minutes, I dried, and Mom cut my hair.

Although I felt better, a tiny bit of uncertainty left traces of edginess under my skin. Adding to it, memories raced through my mind. Trapped in the nail chair, solving riddles, the cold snapping my feet, encountering the hideous demon, how it poured disgustingly frigid water on me, its loud and smelly howl, the unclear words, the bizarre tilts and swirling of reality. Twitching at the horrid memories, my jaw quivered.

I saw the demon in the mirror behind me.

"What's wrong, sweetie?"

The creature disappeared. Taking a huge breath, I searched for the right words. "I'm …" finding an honest answer, I nodded. "Remembering what it was like when…we were separated." I paused. "It was…

horrible.” I darted glances at the mirror – but the demon never returned.

“It’s gone now, okay?” She kissed me on the forehead and dusted off the clipped hair of my neck and shoulders.

One memory stood out – and it made me wonder. “Mom … you played ‘Home Sweet Home’ a lot while that thing had a hold of me – didn’t you?”

She smiled and nodded. “Every day. Why? Did you hear me.”

Barely nodding, I confirmed her question. “Yes – a few times. I followed it, trying to find you.”

She lifted my chin so I could face her.

“You did.”

“I … looked for dad when I was in there.” I shook my head. “I couldn’t find him.”

She put her arm around my shoulders and pulled tightly. “I know you miss him. I miss him, too. But when I look into your eyes, I see your father’s eyes. I see a boy becoming a man like my husband. He was so proud of you and loved you so much – and I love you, too.” She kissed my cheek. “I’ll be here for you as long as I live.”

Mom’s words released the chains that linked me to the heavy fear and doubt – leaving me free and unencumbered. Even the room seemed brighter.

Letting go of Dad, I kept the only thing remaining of him: fond memories of us working on engines, going to baseball and football games, and watching classic horror movies.

I felt renewed putting on a T-shirt that was now too big for me. Although the warm jacuzzi water calmed the numb pain in my joints and muscles, they still had a touch of discomfort as I moved – grunting with every step. I laughed because I had to pull my boxers and shorts up every few steps because I had lost so much weight.

Turning towards the kitchen, I gasped at the sight. Startled, I stopped at the darkened kitchen, seeing shadows that pivoted their heads while whispering. A cold dread wrapped around me. I felt nervous, as my stomach knotted, and my heart raced. Realizing it came back with others, I hastily stepped back.

"Surprise!" Lights flickered on, revealing Father Matthew, Sister Regina, Aunt Beth, Gunner, and Elise. "Happy Birthday," they all yelled.

Relieved, I let out a huge smile and sighed as they gathered around me. The peace and love grew inside my chest, warming it from the fearful chill. Even more comforting were their hands that touched my shoulders, back, and neck. Content, happy, I sensed a peace spread around me like a sleeping bag that protected me from the cold. "Thank-you." I repeated my appreciation several times as tears poured out the underside of my eyes.

My smile spread more – hurting my cheeks when I saw the Choffe Cake with candles in it. My grandma on Dad's side made it for us when she was alive. It was the most delicious cake with the perfect icing, and texture. Although it was mostly chocolate and sugar, Grandma used coffee as a huge ingredient – so we combined "chocolate" and 'coffee' into "Choffe Cake.

My smile faded when I realized this cake was for my birthday – and Elise's. I dropped my head, realizing it was March 17. Dad said Elise and me being born on St. Patrick's Day insulted our Scottish Lineage. He also joked how we should find another Catholic Church not named for St. Patrick.

Stunned, I stared at the cake for a moment. Everyone quieted.

"Jeffrey? What is it?" Mom asked.

I gulped hard. My eyes looked at Father Matthew. "It's March 17?" I had to think about it. "I…missed…three months…of my life? That's how long it had a hold of me?"

"Jeffrey," said Father Matthew, "the important thing is you're back."

"And it's gone," said Mom.

Gunner clasped my shoulder, turning me to face him. I never saw his eyes so full of emotion. "Jeffrey – you're my best friend and I was worried sick I'd never see you again. I don't know what we all would've done without you. So, dude, don't worry about how long you were gone, okay? Just be glad you're back because we all missed you so much."

I grinned, happy to see them all again. I remembered being worried I'd never see them again.

Elise lit the candles on the cake.

"It's your birthday too," I said. "We both gotta blow 'em out like we've always done."

"I know." Her face remained unemotional as she kissed me on the cheek. "But today we celebrate you."

Freddy appeared at my feet, barking for my attention. Seeing his tail wag as he placed his front paws on my thighs, I stooped to pet him. My dog likes me again! "I missed you, Freddy." He licked my cheek and nose, then rolled on his back. I knew what he wanted – so I rubbed his belly.

We all sat at the large dining table, and everyone sang "Happy Birthday" to me and Elise. Mom and Aunt Beth cooked the waffles, eggs, and bacon and we all enjoyed eating and talking with each other for the longest time. It was the best meal I ever had, probably because I was with the people I loved the most.

At one point, I struggled to raise my voice to get Father Matthew's attention. It still sounded scratchy and weak. "Father?" He acknowledged me. "That … thing won't come back, right?"

He shook his head to reiterate his answer. "No. It should not come back."

Blowing out a breath calmed the one bit of fear the demon left in me. "Why do demons possess people like that?" I asked.

Father Matthew hesitated. I could tell he thought hard about my question, which told me he cared enough to give me a satisfactory answer. "Nobody really knows. However, I think its goal is to pass on its own despair to people. It knows in the end it will be locked in the abyss. It's trying to spread its own dread and fear, to convince us that God does not love us."

Elise turned to me. "What's it like under its control? Do you remember anything?"

It seemed like the entire world stopped to focus on me, waiting for my answer with heavy anticipation. I narrowed my eyelids to think about it and find my answer. "Actually," I hesitated. "I don't remember anything." My voice trailed.

Mom broke the uneasy silence that lingered. "Let's not talk about that – or even think about things like that for a while. It's gone. So, let's celebrate and discuss good things – like birthdays and what's ahead for the family."

"Amen," said Father Matthew.

"Amen!"

I couldn't believe even Elise said it with such enthusiasm, even though she still didn't smile.

Lullaby

I crawled into bed. The fresh sheets felt so wonderful that I pulled the quilt tight, helping me feel safe and secure. A healing quality soothed the pain in my body. What remained of fear and uncertainty exited my lungs, broke into fine particles, and faded into nothingness. I inhaled, taking in all the good surrounding me.

Looking around my room – I couldn't believe it. There were several cracks and holes in the drywall – and some had blood stains. A few windows had cracks and had tape over them. Even the ceiling had some damage – mostly cracks and a couple of holes. Some bookshelves had collapsed. Some of my trophies and collectibles had been damaged. I noticed the pictures of family and friends were all cracked.

I kept wondering if that demon would ever come back. Father Matthew said it should not be back. According to him, the proper exorcism condemns it to Hell, locking it in eternity.

The contented feeling wrapped around me. For the first time in … sheesh I'm not sure how long … I felt at ease. Some sort of other feeling warmed my stomach and chest. It was hard to pinpoint, or even describe. Love, perhaps?

Freddy hopped onto the mattress with me and curled into a little ball near my feet. I heard him yawn as I turned out the lights. "Good night, Freddy. Good night, Gunner."

I'm glad he could stay the night – feeling a little scared about the demon returning. The assurance of Father Matthew, though convincing, did not snuff out all the doubt and fear. Again, I apologized to Gunner for hurting him – probably for the hundredth time.

"Good-night, Cuz."

He crawled on the carpeted floor and under some blankets. Usually, we'd talk for a while, but tonight, I wanted to sleep peacefully. I hoped the rest would alleviate the pain in my muscles and joints.

I pulled the covers up to my shoulder. My insides shook a little bit. My smile faded, realizing I had betrayed my family because I lied to everyone. I wish I didn't, but … I remembered everything that happened.

I woke up. Feeling uneasy, I glanced around my room. Nothing but darkness. The gentle "tick-tock" sound was the only thing that moved through the air. I pulled the blankets off and stood. The door hinge creaked slightly, indicating it needed some WD-40. My eyes scanned to the left, focusing on Jeffrey's room. Glad he was back, I barely smiled.

The floor was chilly, but a starker cold wrapped around me – freezing the tip of my nose and chilling my ears.

In Jeffrey's room, I stared at my brother lying in bed. He looked so peaceful. His calm breaths found a perfect rhythm. Again, I smiled … sort of.

My eyes dropped to the left, staring at Gunner's shadow. A vile, bitter hatred swelled like a huge wave that bubbled from volcanic eruptions. Confused, I did not know where it came from or why it spoke to me. So powerful, the angry resentment swelled in my chest. The voice got louder, stronger, and compelling. An irksome ringing erupted – annoying my ears.

Tempted, I flexed my muscles while clutching the scalpel in my pocket. The vibrations in my ears subsided. Not, yet. I'll have to wait for the right moment to cut off Gunner's dick and balls. Maybe that will make the voice go away.

About the Author:

Stephen W. Scott was born in Tulsa, OK. He attended the University of Oklahoma and graduated with a degree in Journalism – Professional Writing. He has worked for a few newspapers, then moved to Wilmore, KY in 1991 to attend Asbury Theological Seminary where he received his Master of Divinity in 1995. After returning to Oklahoma, he served as a pastor in the United Methodist Conference. He has been working in education since 2001 and resides in Tulsa, OK. He also wrote "Clone Hunter" (out of print) and "Abandoned." He enjoys bicycling, reading, playing guitar and writing.

www.swscott-author.com